DIPLOMAT AT ARMS

OPERATION MARRAKESH
BOOK 2

BLAZE WARD

KNOTTED ROAD PRESS

Diplomat at Arms
Operation Marrakesh, Book 2
Blaze Ward
Copyright © 2024 Blaze Ward
All rights reserved
Published by Knotted Road Press
www.KnottedRoadPress.com

ISBN: 978-1-64470-398-4

Cover art:
ID 126123651 © Freestyleimages | Dreamstime.com

Cover and interior design copyright © 2024 Knotted Road Press

Reviews

It's true. Reviews help. Even a short one, such as, "Loved it!" So please consider reviewing this book (and all of the ones you've read) on your favorite retailer site.

Never miss a release!

If you'd like to be notified of new releases, sign up for my newsletter.

http://www.blazeward.com/newsletter/

Buy More!

Did you know that you can buy directly from the Knotted Road Press website?

https://www.knottedroadpress.com/shop/

ALSO BY BLAZE WARD

The Jessica Keller Chronicles

Auberon

Queen of the Pirates

Last of the Immortals

Goddess of War

Flight of the Blackbird

The Red Admiral

St. Legier

Winterhome

Petron

CS-405

Queen Anne's Revenge

Packmule

Persephone

First Centurion Kosnett

Encounter at Vilahana

Consensus at Aditi

Hegemony at Dalou

Princes at Ewin

Empire at Gloran

Domain at Yaumgan

Additional Alexandria Station Stories

The Story Road

Siren

Two Bottles of Wine With A War God

The Science Officer Series Season One

The Science Officer

The Mind Field

The Gilded Cage

The Pleasure Dome

The Doomsday Vault

The Last Flagship

The Hammerfield Gambit

The Hammerfield Payoff

The Bryce Connection

The Science Officer Series Season Two

Alien Seas

Buried Among the Stars

Captain Navarre

Last Stand

Lost Dreams

Ghost Towns

Games People Play

Prophet and Loss

Dandelion

Emergency

Warchild

Moot

Doomsday Girl

Princess

The Coven

Preacher Man

Captain Daring

Revoked

Returned

Reborn

The Lazarus Alliance

Escape

Return

Rebellion

Revolution

Liberation

Retribution

Alliance

Shadow of the Dominion

Longshot Hypothesis

Hard Bargain

Outermost

Dominion-427

Phoenix

Princess Rualoh

PRELUDE

Log: Directorate Cruiser, Tactical Transport
    Marrakesh (CTT)
Station: Monsanch (Unaffiliated)
Attached Special Mission Modules:
A + B) Starliner Double Pod
Mission: Diplomatic Transport Mission to
    Monsanch
Project: R23-T5A25N77
Security Clearance: 2

1

Padraig surveyed the room with perhaps a more jaundiced eye than the situation called for, but he was hardly a diplomatic expert. Merely the captain that had delivered an *A'Zedi* ambassador to Monsanch for this mission.

The music was nice, a six-piece orchestral ensemble playing quietly in a corner. Perhaps as many as a hundred people standing around dressed fancy while chatting quietly, loud by multiplication rather than emotion. The large hall seemed to swallow a lot of the noise.

A cocktail party. Which was not the sort of thing Captain Boru had ever grown accustomed to.

On the one hand, having his Tactical Transport *Marrakesh* hauling the ambassador all the way out here might be construed by some of the locals as something of an insult, as she had not traveled aboard a proper cruiser or Ship of the Line. At the same time, she traveled in far greater style, having arrived aboard one of the nicest double Starliner Pods that Padraig had ever seen.

It had almost been like plugging in a small, five-star hotel for her and her staff, including two separate restaurants that had hosted a few meals for Padraig and some of his officers, largely by lottery as they didn't have the resources to handle the full plague of locusts of the rest of the enlisted descending on them regularly.

"Ah, there you are, Captain," a voice came up from behind him.

Padraig turned, tugging at his dress uniform as he did. He needed to see about having it taken in in a few places and let out in others, as he'd been busy so much lately that he'd stopped eating as many calories. Or sitting behind a desk as much.

Forever moving about, making sure *Marrakesh* was ready to go.

It was not the oldest ship in commission, but it was the last of the M-class cruiser hulls still serving, with the fleet up to O- and even a few P-class cruisers built these days.

At the same time, he was a cruiser captain several years ahead of where he'd expected to be, as a result of the war that had broken out again, getting promoted almost literally from Knight to Captain in a single bound, with only a month as a Commander in between.

Padraig fixed a vacuous, welcoming smile on his face as he completed the turn.

Governor Hesell himself. Head of Government for Monsanch. Tall man. Gladhander. Smart had been Padraig's impression.

A man who got shit done.

A'Zedi Ambassador Sana Alkes should be around here. And should have been dealing with the Governor. Padraig was just the transport section.

Still, he was on stage. Dressed nice and everything. Hair cut two days ago. Freshly shaved before coming down in the transport pod *Roadrunner* to the surface of the planet.

Standing around with a glass of white wine in one hand that wasn't at all to his taste. Too sour. He'd have gone for a port, or possibly a mild Malbec, but he'd taken what the steward had on her tray.

"Governor," Padraig nodded amiably.

He had a few of his more-junior officers attending, with his First Officer aboard the ship in command, but mostly it was the Ambassador's staff. And a bevy of locals in a variety of fashions.

"What do you think of our little party, Captain?" the Governor asked brightly. Leadingly, even.

Padraig paused and took a sip of the sour/tart wine to buy time as he looked around. Folks seemed relaxed. Behaving, at least, which was really all he cared about.

"It seems successful, sir," Padraig replied evenly, turning his attention fully back to the man.

Tall and quite handsome. Lighter skinned than Padraig or much of his crew, though not as pale as some colonies. Brown hair more reminiscent of *Wronlori* than *A'Zedi*, though.

"I understand from Ambassador Alkes that you've had some excitement and adventures lately, Captain Boru?" Hesell continued, eyes big and attentive.

Padraig shrugged. That was one way to describe it, though not the one he'd have chosen, given a thesaurus in hand.

"As with many things, we didn't start it," Padraig replied, smiling up at the man.

Up. Not many men were taller than his one hundred and eighty-six centimeters. Hesell had perhaps four on him. Useful, for a politician.

"But you did finish it, from what Alkes mentioned," Hesell smiled.

Padraig kept the grimace mostly off his face.

"A *Wronlori* Leviathan came out of Ghost-space looking for trouble, sir," Padraig replied simply. "We got lucky and drove them off with damage, then returned home for a quick refit. From there, a Starliner and an Ambassador, and here we are, sir."

Hesell nodded.

"Significant damage done, I gather?" he asked, one eyebrow raised.

"I have a good crew, Governor," Padraig replied.

"So now you've come to Monsanch with your troubles, Captain?" Hesell asked.

His tone was light, as were his hazel eyes, but Padraig wasn't fooled. Nor by the wry smile appearing and disappearing on his mouth like smoke.

Ambassador Alkes was a career ambassador, so definitely not someone you played poker with. Padraig supposed that he might be the best target if the Governor wanted to pump somebody for information.

Fortunately, he didn't really know that much, as he'd spent much of the last year working up *Marrakesh* for operations, training his crew, and now bringing them out on a second major mission.

"No," Padraig replied firmly.

"No?" Hesell pressed.

"Partly, *A'Zedi*'s needs are driven by geography, Governor Hesell," Padraig replied with a nod. "As you no doubt are aware. With *Wronlori* more or less spinward and *Copez* anti-spinward, plus *Traisa* more towards the galactic rim, *A'Zedi* mostly has an open border coreward. Thus, we explore more this direction. And meet folks like you, whose ancestors migrated closer to the galactic core many centuries ago. Plus, *Wronlori* has started the last several wars, so personally, I'd admonish them for a failure to behave."

Padraig finished off his wine to give himself a reason to stop talking. And perhaps look for a new glass of something more palatable. Even fruit juice would be an improvement.

Hesell had a slight smile on his face. Not superior. Knowing, perhaps.

Padraig smiled and shrugged just enough to be obvious in the way his shoulders moved.

Idly, Padraig wondered about the Governor's sexuality. He generally classified himself ninety/ten queer. Not opposed to women, but very few caught his attention for even a second look.

Even Ambassador Alkes—dark, curvy, and lush as one might expect more from a teenage boy drawing cheesecake art —didn't really draw Padraig's eye, save that few women he'd known with hips and chest like that still managed a trim waist between them.

Hesell had a gleam in his eyes that Padraig found... *interesting*.

It would be hilarious if Command had thrown Alkes at the man, only to have her bounce off for reasons similar to Padraig's. And that seemed to be the look in the man's eyes.

Most interesting.

They paused, staring almost awkwardly at one another. Padraig had been all set to excuse himself, that he might find another glass, but something in Hesell's eyes held him in place.

Then an aide slipped in behind Hesell, covered the man's ear, and whispered something.

Padraig pretended to study a distant picture, but still

caught the flinch of surprise that rippled thtough Hesell's muscular frame. The way those hazel eyes suddenly got huge, before narrowing with what looked like rage. The firm set of the jaw, not quite chewing nails but not far short. Weight rolled forward onto the balls of his feet as though combat might be imminent.

Padraig shifted his perception and looked for a better weapon than a broken-off wine glass, though that and fists might have to do.

"Where?" Hesell demanded of the newcomer.

The man nodded back over his shoulder, panic evident in his face, though Hesell was better at hiding it.

"You'll pardon me, Captain Boru?" Governor Hesell nodded. "A situation has arisen that demands my immediate attention."

"Of course, sir," Padraig replied, but he was already looking at the man's back.

Shoulders forward and down. A tread like a giant stomping ant hills as he passed.

Someone was about to have an exceptionally bad day. Padraig was happy that it would be someone else, from the way Governor Hesell had responded.

He noted Ambassador Alkes emerge from the crowd nearby and make her way closer.

Utterly beautiful woman. Medium height but broad in shoulders and hips like an hourglass. Long black hair down and wavy. Skin a few shades lighter in hue. Ambassadorial robes that had been modified to show off her curves and plunge low at her decolletage, a fine platinum chain with a blue stone, showing off the rich bronze of her skin, only a few shades darker than Padraig's.

Black eyes laughing at some inner joke.

Padraig more bowed to her than nodded. He was merely the captain of her transport. She was the Ambassador traveling to Monsanch.

Before she could speak, someone screamed.

2

Padraig turned and prepared for battle, but nothing threatened.

Still, he had the wine glass. It would make a useful opening move, then he'd be back to his hand-to-hand training.

Except that nothing threatened.

Hesell had made it as far as the doorway, but stopped and turned back to the room. It helped that he was the second or third tallest person visible, so Padraig had been able to follow his progress through the crowd.

The Governor turned now and raised both hands above his head.

"If I could have your attention, please!" he roared in a voice that stilled crowd and musicians alike.

Like a pond on a cool, winter morning as the fog is just starting to burn off.

"Ladies and gentlemen, this reception must, I am sorry, end immediately," Hesell continued. "My apologies, but a situation has arisen that requires my attention. If you would make your orderly way to the exits, there will be more news shortly."

Padraig turned to Alkes, but she met his glance with a shrug.

"What just happened, Boru?" she asked.

"One of Hesell's aides whispered in his ear," Padraig replied. "He immediately set off, but only got that far. Should we inject ourselves into the situation, or withdraw?"

She studied him closer. Almost undressed him with her eyes, but they both already knew that she wasn't his type.

Hesell's?

"We are still outsiders here," she decided after a moment. "Let us withdraw to your ship for now. This mission does not have to be concluded in a day."

Padraig nodded and reached into a pocket inside his over-shirt for a transmitter, keying it live.

"*Marrakesh*. Messier," Chance replied instantly.

But then, his First Officer didn't have much to do up in orbit, save wait for something to happen.

Something apparently had.

"Boru," he replied. "Let the Air Boss know that we'll be returning to *Roadrunner* shortly. I'm not sure if we're staying planetside or returning to the ship just yet, but the party just ended quite abruptly and you should bump your alert level a notch, just in case."

"We expecting trouble, Padraig?" she asked.

"Expecting?" he replied. "No. It might come looking, though."

"Roger that," she agreed. "*Roadrunner* is warm and standing by for you."

"Good work, Chance," he said. "Stand by for an update as soon as I know anything."

He killed the line and turned to Alkes. Several of her folks had migrated inward to pool around her, just as Kaitlin Lynch, his Stevedore aboard *Marrakesh*, had done the same.

Around them, locals were slowly filing towards the exits, like someone had pulled the plug on a tub of water.

He let the rest have a head start before following. They were among the last to make it to the door when that same aide slipped close and tugged on Padraig's sleeve.

"Sir," he said. "The Governor asks that you and the Ambassador remain behind, that he can brief you in person shortly."

Padraig looked to Alkes. Her mission.

She nodded a moment later, so Padraig turned to Kaitlin.

"You get folks to *Roadrunner*," he ordered. "Hang tight on the ground until we know what's going on and where you should take them."

Kaitlin nodded and took charge. That was mostly what a ship's Stevedore did, at least on a Tactical Transport. She was responsible for the two modular slots—currently occupied by the double Starliner pod—as well as the people that usually came with such things. Diplomats in this case.

And had served the *A'Zedi* navy as an enlisted crew member for thirty years before retiring, then returned to harness as a civilian technical specialist for *Marrakesh*, rather than accepting a commission.

Still one of the best he'd ever known.

The groups fragmented, and he found himself standing next to the aide and Alkes as the rest kept going.

"Where to?" Padraig asked.

"This way," the man nodded, turning and leading them down a side corridor currently empty.

Padraig focused on memorizing where they were going.

Sounded like it was going to be a long night.

3

Kaitlin was used to herding goldfish. Some people compared her job to herding cats, but cats didn't move in three dimensions. Goldfish were a bigger pain in the ass. And more accurate here.

Still, none of the Ambassador's folks wandered off to the point that she needed to snap at them.

Kaitlin had no idea what was going on. The one woman who had screamed had immediately fainted, but Kaitlin hadn't known who she was. Then the Governor got directly involved and cleared decks.

At least Padraig would be remaining behind.

She'd known a lot of commanding officers in her time. Few of them stacked up well against Boru, even as young as he was. That just meant that he was likely to get even better with a few more years of seasoning.

She could see him in the uniform of a Fleet Marshal one of these days.

"Ma'am, what should we be doing?" a woman from Alkes's staff asked.

"Out and across the back patio to the landing grid," Kaitlin replied. "*Roadrunner* has enough space for everyone, plus a head and a kitchenette in case you need it. I expect that we'll know what's happening in an hour or so. At that point, we return to *Marrakesh* or transport directly to the hotel via locals."

They'd only been in system for three days. Long enough to arrive and dance over the comm with locals. Then arrange a reception for Alkes, with Kaitlin and Padraig along as make-weights more than anything.

The hotel was ready for them, but they hadn't even checked in yet, expecting that to occur later this evening. After a successful party.

Still, she could keep this mob sorted and organized. They'd been pretty easy company on the flight out here.

Kaitlin smiled and made sure none of her goldfish got lost as they headed towards the back doors of the palace.

4

Padraig studied the room they'd ended up in. Not quite an office. Not really a personal suite. Maybe a day room? It reminded him of a similar space off *Marrakesh*'s bridge, where his crew could take a break to get coffee or stretch, in the middle of a long shift.

Couple of working-style tables in the middle, with a couch and several chairs of various softness levels visible. Bookshelves and plants in pots. Art on the walls that looked to be mostly portraits of folks he didn't know, in outfits a historian might be able to identify.

Or not.

They were a lot of light-years away from Horwin, capital world of the *A'Zedi Directorate*.

Padraig found a coffee robot in a nearby cabinet and dialed himself a mug. It felt like maybe the late afternoon was about to turn into a long night, and he was still adjusting to planetary time, nearly nine hours ahead of *Marrakesh*'s clock.

Alkes joined him a moment later, close enough that he could feel her heat, standing next to him.

He glanced over at the shorter woman. Most women were shorter, so he was used to it. Few were as perfectly beautiful, though it really didn't do anything for him.

"The woman who screamed," she murmured. "I was facing the wrong direction. Do you remember who she was? She collapsed too quickly for me to see her."

Padraig nodded and replayed the moment in his mind, picking out her face from the crowd of more than one hundred folks he'd at least smiled at in passing as he went.

Utterly pale skin, with hair like spun gold, even lighter than *Wronlori*.

"*Traisa* in origin," he muttered. "I think she might have been the wife of their Ambassador, though I only saw her in passing, rather than part of the meet and greet line."

Hesell hadn't gone all in on the pomp of everyone walking a line to shake his hand. Instead, major players had been pointed out for a quick hello, but even then Padraig had largely stayed off to one side.

Not aloof, but not a *player* as these people measured things. Merely the driver, if he could be so rude.

"Eliana Wrezal," Alkes nodded now. "Yes, that was her. Indeed she is his wife. Did you see him in the mob at the end?"

Padraig would have liked to have had an eidetic memory, able to see everything as a series of scans or photographs, but he had not been so blessed.

"I did not," he replied as the coffee robot disgorged its first mug before starting on the next one. "Is that important?"

"Unknown, Captain," the Ambassador replied. "Presumably, Governor Hesell will be more forthcoming soon."

A door opened at the far end of the room and Hesell stepped though, pausing to mutter something inaudible to someone outside before closing it.

The three of them were alone.

The coffee robot completed a second pass and disgorged Alkes's mug as Hesell stepped close.

"That sounds like a good idea," the Governor said, nodding to himself as he pressed a few buttons.

Alkes had taken a full steo backwards, in the process boxing Padraig in before he was able to do the same.

Throwing him at the Governor?

Hesell turned as the machine whirred and ground.

"There has been a murder," he announced simply, skipping all the diplomatic niceties that might otherwise require fifteen minutes to actually mention the key parts.

Burying the lede, as it were. Or exactly the opposite, in this case.

"Sir?" Padraig asked in his apparent role as straight man today.

"The *Traisa* Ambassador, Joshua Wrezal," Hesell continued. "Someone killed him in a side room and left the body, but he was alone when discovered."

"I see," Padraig replied, uncertain as to what Hesell was implying.

Or not implying.

"What should we do, Governor?" Padraig finally asked, since Sana Alkes had pushed him into the line of fire.

Probably wise, as any mistakes would be on his head, and she could step in and smooth things over later. Or chew his ass out publicly as necessary for the success of *her mission*.

"What is your relationship with *Traisa*, Captain?" Hesell asked.

Padraig rocked back onto his heels to think. And sipped some coffee.

The Governor obviously got a better selection of beans than a third-tier Tactical Transport did. Good stuff.

"We—being the *Sovereign Collective Directorate of A'Zedi*—are currently engaged in what modern historians are calling the *War of the Fourth Alliance*, being *A'Zedi* and our ally, the *Holy Imperium of Copez*, against what might be classified as our traditional foe at this point, the *United Technocracy*, also known as *Wronlori* for their original culture. *Traisa*—the so-called *Enlightened Tyranny*—is generally neutral this time around, at least far as I know, but I'm also merely a ship's captain, and not any sort of important diplomat entrusted with such information by Command."

He nodded to Sana Alkes as he said that last part, reminding the Governor that she was the hotshot here. The *A'Zedi* Ambassador sent specifically to Monsanch to see if she could negotiate any sort of deal with the locals.

Monsanch was an *Unaffiliated World*. There were a lot of those, dating back many centuries to when Ghostdrives first got small enough and cheap enough that a group of a thousand or so colonists with good bloodlines and medical science could set off and establish their own colony on some world.

There were many such empty worlds out there. Generally lacking anything higher than primitive animal forms, to say nothing of intelligent life, but adequate if you brought enough things with you across the stars.

"And Ambassador Wrezal?" Hesell asked, practically ignoring Alkes and all the openings Padraig was giving her to step in.

Please?

"I'd never even heard of him until we arrived in-system and got the guest list for your event, Governor," Padraig answered honestly. "First I met him was to shake his hand a few hours ago. Did the man have enemies?"

There, toss it back into Hesell's lap and force him to make accusations. Or wherever he was driving things.

"The wars of the exterior rarely impinge on our lives out here, Captain Boru," Hesell replied in a steely voice.

"Then you should probably count yourself lucky, Governor," Padraig said. "Monsanch occupies a most interesting location in the galaxy, being far enough away from everyone that you are surrounded by neutral space, while at the same time, sitting on the rimward edge of a sector of the galaxy where the stars get dense. Good place for folks to settle. Compact enough that I could see another star nation forming there over the next few generations, depending. Personally, I doubt it, but it might happen."

"Why do you doubt it, Boru?" Hesell asked, eyes narrowing as he turned to more fully face Padraig.

"The thing that struck me most about folks I met this afternoon was your culture's rugged individualism, sir," Padraig nodded. "Still close to those original colonists that struck out into the interior to leave everyone behind, at least socially. You wouldn't want to be part of something else, unless you drove it yourself from Monsanch. Or did it defensively because everyone else was starting to annoy you."

"And is *A'Zedi* going to annoy us?" Hesell asked, turning his eyes sharply to Alkes for once and letting Padraig duck having to answer *that sort of question.*

"We're here to establish trade and cultural ties, Governor," she replied in a soothing, radio voice that was exactly the kind you wanted seducing you on a dark night with a glass of good port in one hand and a hologram of a fire burning nearby.

Assuming you liked women.

"To the detriment of *Traisa*?" Hesell ground on.

"Hardly," she retorted, adding a bit of sharpness to her voice now. "The *Enlightened Tyranny* is generally at least friendly with *A'Zedi* these days. I hesitate to cast aspersions on them without meeting them in the flesh first, but my first assumption would be to investigate your *Wronlori* Ambassador. I noted that she did not attend this event, presumably to keep her and I from having to meet for the first time in a large, public setting where you might not be able to control emotions. Thank you for that, by the way. I'd like to meet her at some point where it might be a handful of us to chat over tea, if that's an acceptable next step as you work to understand what happened here."

Padraig nodded, which unfortunately reminded Hesell that he was still here, as the taller man's eyes slid back and speared his.

"*Wronlori*?" Hesell asked in a quieter-but-no-less-deadly voice.

Padraig shrugged carefully.

"I am probably the wrong person to ask, Governor," he said. "Personally, I've had recent, unpleasant dealings with their fleet, but that was a military thing, entirely unrelated to the diplomatic business at hand. As we were discussing before all this went wrong, they started it at Albany. I have a good crew on *Marrakesh*, and we finished it. At the same time, I would be highly surprised if they immediately sent orders to Monsanch to continue such shenanigans on my behest, as *Marrakesh* is not the pride or flagship of the *A'Zedi* fleet. We're a Tactical Transport, and I'm a nobody captain. Make of that what you will."

That seemed to be the right tone, as Hesell relaxed. His weight shifted back off his toes and his head came up again.

Padraig did the same, aware that things were close to out of hand.

And that Sana had let them get there.

Not the time to demand explanations from her, either. That would be back on his ship.

Where he was in charge.

"Yes," Governor Hesell nodded after a moment. "I've sent everyone home, as most of the people present work for me and the rest were accredited to various embassies. Holding them all here while detectives investigated things would send the wrong message. And likely would insult a few of them unnecessarily."

"How can I—we—help, sir?" Padraig asked.

"Don't take any of this personal, Captain," Hesell replied, nodding over his shoulder to the Ambassador as well. "There will be a police investigation, but it will be complicated by the fact that everyone has some level of diplomatic immunity."

"Understood, Governor," Padraig said. "Should my people return to the ship, or remain on the surface for the next few days while things get sorted out?"

Again, the tall man paused. Studied something ten thousand light-years away over Padraig's shoulder, but it wasn't the amazingly beautiful woman standing there.

"Return to your ship, Captain, Ambassador," Hesell nodded. "Then we might have another event and reset the clock, as it were. It is my hope that perhaps Wrezal was simply done in by a jealous lover somewhere."

"Did he have that sort of reputation, sir?" Padraig asked.

"Oh, indeed," Hesell nodded, turning to go with a smile on his face. "The man was a scoundrel."

5

Kaitlin studied Padraig's face as he boarded *Roadrunner*. Stress. Concern. Confusion.

But still the Captain. That was good.

"Gather round, folks," he said as the hatch closed. "Air Boss, we're returning to *Marrakesh* directly."

Kaitlin nodded. Something had happened, but they were getting out of the line of fire. That was also good.

Padraig turned to Sana. Ambassador Alkes, but she and Kaitlin had had time to relax and chat some on a personal level, during the flight out. Part of her job as Stevedore. Part of Sana's job as Ambassador.

Learning that Padraig wouldn't be at all interested had surprised the woman, but likely saved a few awkward moments later. Sana liked being the center of attention and frequently dressed a bit provocatively. Kaitlin preferred being comfortable.

Alkes stepped up now and gathered folks. Nine of them, including a couple of Padraig's folks mostly along to run messages and stuff. He and Sana had been the stars of the show, as far as Kaitlin was concerned.

"You will keep this quiet, but I don't imagine that it won't come out fairly quickly," Sana told the assembled group. "The *Traisa* Ambassador is dead. It looks on first blush like an assassination, but we don't have any more details than that. The Governor wanted us out of his hair while his people investigated things, assuming that we were being set up to look bad by someone. We'll stay aboard *Marrakesh* and do whatever we can from there, so let's keep the hotel reservations but let them know we're delayed on check in."

One of Sana's people nodded from the back and started typing. Kaitlin didn't have to do anything at present except get back to the ship and continue being a Den Mother as Padraig needed it for Sana's staff.

"All hands, please settle in for launch," Air Boss Rafferty called from the flight deck. He'd flown them down personally, rather than letting anyone else have any fun. "Lift off in twenty seconds."

Jump seats got folded down and folks strapped themselves in quickly. Even civilians had learned that Walt wasn't kidding when he gave you a countdown.

Kaitlin made sure she was on Padraig's far side from Sana, so all the conversations went through him.

"What do you need, Sana?" she asked as her boss listened.

"Presumably, you will go ahead with resupply," Sana replied. "And maybe sooner rather than later, since we were expecting to be on the surface instead of eating up there. I may return to the surface quietly to interface with the Governor, but not for a few days. I'd rather not be that one thing too many right at the moment."

"Gotcha," Kaitlin said. "I already have bids out for things, so adding some extra fresh food won't be a problem. Do we expect anything beyond diplomatic turmoil?"

She was looking at Padraig when she asked.

"We'll ask Chance when we get there," he replied some-what evasively. "Governor Hesell called the *Traisa* Ambassador a scoundrel, but meant it in the way that he might have been killed over jealousy rather anything political. If so, then hope-fully none of it falls on our heads and we can get back to being a simple diplomatic mission to Monsanch."

Kaitlin nodded. There was always the chance that things only looked bad when you applied your own spin on things. Tried to find order in pure chaos, when there really was nothing there.

Roadrunner lifted off with a roar of vectored thrust, sliding forward as Walt moved them towards a launch corridor. *Marrakesh* was above, moving geo-synchronously to the Governor's Palace while they were below.

"Padraig, are there any other ships in orbit we should worry about?" Sana asked.

"None," he shook his head. "We're the only military vessel of any kind, though that could change as soon as news gets out. Especially if the *Enlightened Tyranny* decides that they need to do something. It would take a message probably three days to get to Zulou from here. A ship would then take at least two weeks getting here, even if they were immediately ready to fly and pushed their engines and fuel to the limit."

"Sana, what's the Supreme Autocrat likely to do?" Kaitlin asked.

She watched the woman shrug.

"Diplomatically, I presume that Wrezal has a Deputy who would immediately begin exercising his powers, but under-standing that everything he did was temporary," Sana replied. "Supreme Autocrat Arodd Torray would need to send a replacement, but that might take a month at their end at a minimum."

"Anybody likely to cause trouble during that month?" Kaitlin asked, making sure to keep Padraig's face in view as she did.

As he'd said, the only warship in orbit.

For how long?

His grimace was telling, but only because he had the same thought she did.

"One can only guess," Sana nodded. "We're too new on station to even begin to understand the undercurrents. Then, they will have all been radically altered first by us arriving, and now by Wrezal's murder."

"Someone stirring up the interior?" Padraig asked, turning to the Ambassador.

"It's possible," Sana shrugged. "As you noted with the Governor, Monsanch is something of a doorway to a number of other colonies, mostly younger and farther away from everyone else. It's also the most natural place for *A'Zedi* to expand our influence and later power, with us generally being the closest nation.?

"What does anybody gain by killing the *Traisa* Ambassador, then?" Kaitlin asked.

"That is going to be the thing that we need to figure out," Sana nodded.

6

Padraig was back on his ship. On his bridge. In his chair.

He wasn't going to claim to be superstitious, but he also wasn't going to deny it, either. He felt better here.

Safer, though he'd never admit it.

Marrakesh was where he belonged. Two days back from the surface still waiting for things to settle had only confirmed that in his head.

At the same time, Padraig knew that part of a Captain's job was going down to the surface of various planets to meet with local governments and negotiate deals. He was also quite happy to be hauling a big Starliner pod this time, so that Sana Alkes was responsible for that part.

He'd been looking forward to some sightseeing, mostly because Monsanch was an *Unaffiliated World*, originally colonized by a group of folks from the *Wronlori* region of space. Far lighter skin and hair than Padraig or most of *A'Zedi*. Almost pale. All the region variances that humanity represented.

Several worlds claimed to be the original home of humanity, but after this long, nobody was really certain which was. Wars had lifted and overthrown so many republics and empires that much of the evidence was gone.

He'd been looking forward to playing tourist. Now, he might be stuck here on the ship.

And he might not. Padraig had gotten the impression from Governor Hesell that they'd only be back on *Marrakesh* for a week at most while locals investigated the Ambassador's death and dealt with it.

His *A'Zedi* mission certainly wasn't up for blame, having only been here three days, and having landed on the planet then gone directly to the reception at the palace.

Hopefully, nobody believed that he or Sana Alkes were that level of criminal mastermind.

Padraig looked around at the folks on duty with him.

Squire Nyssa Taggart as Radio Officer, in charge of communications and sensors. Not much to do at present, but always working. Always studying.

Nineteen going on fifty. She'd enlisted at seventeen, then been talked into going to Officer Candidate School when folks realized how brilliant she was. Third-youngest crew member aboard. Youngest officer by far. Probably one of the smartest, as well.

Nyssa must have felt his gaze, as she looked up at him expectantly.

"Sir?" she asked, brown eyes locked on.

As with most days, she'd buzzed her brown hair as short as regulations would allow. Maybe one of these days he would let her go ahead and shave it completely.

It was worth keeping her happy.

"What's communications traffic like, Taggart?" Padraig asked pensively.

"It spiked hard after the assassination, sir," she nodded. "Since then, it has remained twenty percent higher than it was on the day before. Right now, running comparable to where it first settled after *Marrakesh* entered the system."

Padraig nodded.

His arrival had been something of a *fox in the hen house* moment. Technically a warship, in a neutral system, but not really a threat. The planet had some level of defenses, but mostly against pirates and bandits.

Nothing that could hold off a serious invasion.

At the same time, it was practically impossible to sail across space and land enough troops on any planet to hold it.

Fleets would settle in orbital space and issue demands instead.

"How encrypted have things been?" he pursued.

"Fifty/fifty, sir," Nyssa replied. "I assume some amount of the coded messages we have detected are diplomatic in nature, everyone sending updates to their own capitals as we have been doing."

"Anything we've been able to crack and read?" Padraig asked, leaning forward.

Nyssa Taggart looked at him with confusion.

"Sir?"

"Codes, Squire," he nodded. "Strings of information rearranged in such a way that they cannot be immediately read. At the same time, they have to contain something for someone at the other end to understand how to read them."

She blinked, then understanding dawned.

"Should I contact the Ambassador for assistance, Captain?" she asked. "Or borrow the navigation computers for now?"

Padraig smiled.

"Let's keep this on a military level currently, Taggart," he replied. "You see what you can do with those tools, so that anything we find can be added to her mission later. Or not, if that would compromise us. Ambassador Alkes needs to be respected by the locals."

"Understood, sir," Nyssa replied brightly.

Her smile suggested another fox in a different hen house, but Padraig wasn't worried.

Monsanch was the middle of nowhere, in many ways.

Unaffiliated. Not poor but there were limits to what you could accomplish with only a single planet forming your economy. Remote and a bit cut off from the main players. Culturally somewhat isolated.

It was entirely possible that someone, somewhere, would transmit a message in an older code that Nyssa could crack. Or someone might transmit an update she intercepted.

He doubted that much would come of it, but wars were won by everyday folks doing the little things that added up into something huge later.

"Sir, I have a message from the ground," she perked up suddenly, touching an earpiece and looking over at him. "The Governor's office is trying to reach you."

"I'll take it in my office," Padraig decided. "You're in charge."

Nyssa was still getting used to that part. The being in command of a starship and crew at nineteen.

She could handle it.

And he'd be all of six steps away if something happened. Plus Chance Messier was aft right now, but should be awake and getting food before coming on duty in a bit.

Starships never slept.

Now, what did the Governor want?

7

Padraig settled behind his desk and brought up the screen. *Marrakesh* was orbiting directly above the capital city of Ilham, so the light-speed lag was infinitesimal.

He keyed the circuit live, noting that it was being encrypted by a code sent to them from the palace when they'd first arrived.

One that had been cracked at some point?

Padraig made a mental note to ask Sana Alkes about delivering a different code that they knew should be impenetrable at present.

Too much subterfuge going around.

Governor Hesell's face filled the screen. He'd shaved and possibly gotten a hair cut in the last two days. Eyes were a little tired, but he looked like he'd gotten enough sleep.

"Governor, how can I help you today?" Padraig asked with a smile on his face.

The man should have called Sana Alkes. Hopefully, this was more formal than a quick chat.

"Captain Boru," Hesell smiled back. "I wanted to ask you a private question."

Padraig kept his face perfectly neutral, regardless of how many different rabbits suddenly broke for the high grass in his mind.

"Sir?"

"You don't seem to have an ax to grind, Captain," Hesell continued. "Did I read that right?"

Padraig paused before speaking, reviewing that last conversation he'd had with the man. Nothing jumped out as problematic, depending on how the man had interpreted things.

"I'm not certain I understand, sir," Padraig hedged his bets.

"You didn't speak of fighting off a *Wronlori* Leviathan with great bravado, Boru," Hesell nodded. "Nor insulting or impugning them, in spite of, as you noted, them starting the last several wars."

"I'm a professional sailor, Governor," Padraig countered. "On a diplomatic mission. It might be Sana Alkes's mission, but I'm here to represent *A'Zedi* and to do so in a good light. I can't convince you to establish better relations with my superiors, but I can damned sure make things worse. Ergo, I must be careful and diplomatic. Doubly so as an outsider."

"That's the reason I wished to speak with you like this, Captain Boru," Hesell nodded. "That outsiderness."

"Sir?"

"You don't bring any specific issues to the table, Captain," the Governor replied. "Even when it didn't matter, you were on your best behavior."

"We're a long ways from home, sir," Padraig said. "And I'm currently the only warship in orbit, however technical that definition. I do expect the others to possibly scramble and send ships, but nobody is likely to be that close, save for any scouts that they might vector down on Monsanch."

"Warships, Captain?" He watched the Governor's entire mien harden down a notch.

"*Marrakesh* arrives, and three days later the *Traisa* Ambassador is murdered?" Padraig replied with a grimace he didn't bother hiding. "Someone might draw the wrong conclusions."

"Indeed, Captain," Hesell nodded, still grim. "What would you suggest?"

"I've been up in orbit, sir, so I don't know the state of the investigation," Padraig said. "Perhaps you should send a message to all capitals via aetherial communications array, letting them know as much as you feel confident revealing at this point. Hopefully, you don't see *Marrakesh* as a threat, so that might allay their concerns, and others don't feel the need to race here madly in order to do something."

Hesell watched him. Padraig watched back.

"Thus, I have a question, Captain," the Governor smiled a moment later.

"Sir."

"I would like you to return to the surface, Captain Boru," Hesell nodded. "You and Sana Alkes, but her in her official capacity, and you as something more of a civilian nature. I'm given to understand that you had intended to play the part of tourist while you were here."

"You are correct, Governor," Padraig said. "Circumstances have somewhat altered that trajectory."

"Indeed, but if you were to return to it, you might be in a position to see or learn things that others might miss."

"Outsider, Governor?" Padraig asked.

"Exactly, Captain," Hesell replied. "Then you can relay things to me. The investigation seems to be going nowhere, to the point that we have several dozen suspects with motive and means, and are no closer to solving this mystery than we were three days ago."

"I'm happy to do what I can, Governor," Padraig nodded. "Not sure how successful I might be, though."

"And I expect you to bring that stubborn confidence with you, Captain," Hesell replied. "You asked how you could help. I need you to break loose things on the surface. Sana Alkes will be polite and beautiful. Delightful in conversation and distracting for most people to look at. I want you to remain somewhat in the background and see what you can find, Captain."

"I'll do what I can, sir," Padraig offered. "But I can't make any promises."

"That's why I asked, Captain."

The line went dead and Padraig leaned back fully into his chair.

Well, that was interesting.

Just how messy were things on the ground?

8

Padraig finished his explanation. Chance Messier, his First Officer, looked at him somewhat askance.

"Really ugly trap?" she asked, then grinned. "Or a quiet way to set the two of you up on a date?"

Padraig snorted. He had no way of knowing the Governor's preferences.

At the same time, there had been a spark the several times they had spoken.

He shrugged.

"We'll see," he temporized. "For now, you'll remain in command up here. I have no idea what Governor Hesell expects me to find, but I'll be moving around in other circles than Sana, so there's a chance that I might actually trip over some clue accidentally."

"You should take Kaitlin down," Chance replied.

Her eyes were intent. Padraig studied the woman who was almost closer to him than a boyfriend in many ways.

Above average height. Average build tending to curvy if she

didn't religiously spend time on the machines and watching her caloric intake. Black hair, but straight.

Her husband Robin was home with the kids, Xandra and Daneel, and she'd finally returned to sailing after flying a desk at headquarters for several years.

"No," he decided. Then had to interrupt Chance's reply. "She can go to the surface, but that's part of her job as Stevedore. We'll need regular resupply, and whatever else comes up. *Marrakesh* is fresh from the yard and a drydock to repair things from that Leviathan, so we should be in good shape mechanically. You'll arrange a rotation for folks to come down to the surface and spend a day in Ilham, but not too many people."

"You need someone with you," Chance insisted. "What about Nyssa?"

"I need her here," Padraig shook his head. "Gave her a quiet mission that requires the nav computers."

"Zarah, then?" Chance pressed. "Might make someone think you took a young, delicate female officer to the surface for *whatever reasons a captain might do such a thing.*"

She said it such a lascivious tone that Padraig found himself blushing anyway. He knew a few officers that maintained quiet relationships aboard a ship, but he never had. And certainly never with someone under his direct command.

Extremely bad for morale.

Still...

"Think they'd fall for it?" he asked. "I realize that Zarah likes to say she's three days out of Uni, but she forgets to mention which school that was. And how well she's been trained."

"She's also much closer in coloration to the locals, Padraig," Chance said. "That might let her disappear, once the two of you are in civilian attire."

"Should I go off duty for this?" he asked, confused. "I had been planning to be in uniform."

Chance got a devious smile on her face. Frightening, even.

"You didn't just spend several years on a desk job doing dirty politics, Padraig," she replied. "Remember, you're dealing with a murderer who killed a man in cold blood. You'll want them to underestimate you at every step. Dressed like a civilian, with a someone who looks like a local girl on your arm, will cause them to draw the wrong conclusions."

"I see," he nodded.

Maybe he did. Chance was a sharp woman. Cunning. *Marrakesh* would be in good hands while he was away, and Zarah didn't need to be flying the ship while they remained in orbit.

"Alright," he said. "Me as a tourist. Her as an aide or some-thing, intended to make them misjudge us both. Any other suggestions, mother?"

He grinned. She grinned back.

"Make sure you stop and enjoy yourself occasionally," Chance nodded. "You are always *on* around here, Padraig. You have earned a little down time."

He nodded back, but didn't feel it. Governor Hesell had asked him to do...something.

What, he wasn't entirely sure, but if it helped *A'Zedi* get a foot in the door, it would be worth it.

"Oh, and watch your back, boss," Chance continued.

Yes, he'd need to do that, as well.

9

Zarah sat awkwardly as the shuttle settled on the surface of Monsanch. Unlike the others, she and Captain Boru—Padraig as he insisted since they were in mufti—had crossed to the main station in orbit, then ridden a commercial, civilian shuttle to the surface.

Much nicer inside than *Roadrunner*, but it was weird, not being in uniform. Especially with the captain next to her.

Still, they'd landed. Her and several dozen others unbuckled and rose.

Zarah looked around the cramped space, still a little surprised at how short the locals tended to be. She stood one hundred and seventy-six centimeters in flats, and at least half the men she could see were shorter than her, along with most of the women.

Padraig Boru was almost a giant at one hundred and eighty-six. But he stood out for his dark color as well, which was just weird for Zarah.

All her life, she'd been pale skinned and had much lighter hair than everyone else she'd known, to the point that she'd been teased about it. Around here, she almost fit in, save for her height.

"You'll be fine, Zarah," Padraig murmured to her, like he could read the edges of panic floating around.

Maybe he could. He was The Captain, after all.

She nodded, gulped once, and reached overhead to draw down the bag she'd packed.

They'd had to draw clothing from the diplomats, because all she had with her were shirts in *A'Zedi* mulberry, and jackets in mauve. She wore her black pants, but had also packed a few other colors they'd given her.

Diplomats had an entire costuming department back there, plus folks with sewing machines to make things on the fly.

She supposed that this might be who she'd have been, had she not decided to join the navy. Black pants, with a green tunic with a brown belt. Padraig wore a kilt in navy blue with a bright red shirt and a gray jacket over it.

He almost looked as much a stranger as she felt.

She'd be fine. They weren't spies. They were tourists. Doing tourist things.

Whatever the hell that meant.

Zarah followed the mob out of the vessel and down a walkway into the landing facility. Folks were getting their papers checked, but a woman Zarah's age in a dark blue uniform waved her and Padraig over to a station on the left with a smile.

"That's the line for locals," she explained as Zarah got close. "Interstellar travelers are here."

"Oh," Zarah nodded, handing the woman her papers. So they knew who she was already.

Padraig did the same.

"Non-business?" the woman asked, consulting a screen Zarah couldn't read.

"My job was delivering the Ambassador," Padraig spoke up cheerfully. "With that completed, I have a few days to myself, so I decided to come down as a civilian and see your world."

Zarah nodded. Completely true.

She did blush when the customs officer eyed her speculatively, but Padraig and Commander Messier had both told her that folks might think the Captain had brought a girlfriend with him to fool around, out of sight of the crew or the ambassador.

She suppressed the snort. Zarah might really like men, but so did Padraig. He was not threat to her.

At the same time, she watched that belief take root.

Huh. It really worked.

She'd been in school learning to be an officer for the last four years, keeping her head down, playing in the orchestra or practicing every spare moment, then immediately assigned to *Marrakesh* on commissioning.

What the hell did she know about normal people's lives?

The woman handed back both sets of docs, stamped, with a knowing smile on her face. Zarah tried to match it, but figured she looked too dorky to pull it off.

She could work with adorable, though. More than one person had told her she'd managed that.

"Welcome to Monsanch," the woman said.

"Thank you," Zarah replied, then they were through and into the main building.

Big and airy. Marble floors. Lots of skylights illuminating the place.

Zarah had her bag over her shoulder, same as Padraig did. She looked up at him expectantly.

"Food, walk, or nap?" he asked.

That took her a moment. Zarah was used to getting orders.

Not being free to do whatever she wanted.

Weird.

Still, green tunic. Him in a kilt.

Off-duty. Or something.

"Food," Zarah decided.

"Following you," he nodded.

Again, her in charge, with the captain walking next to her as she looked for the exit. But he wasn't the captain. He was Padraig, at least for a few days.

She could be Zarah, instead of Squire Halloran off the *A'Zedi* Tactical Transport *Marrakesh*.

Ilham was a major city. Starport wasn't that big, because most of the cargo was handled well outside of town. This space was for people going to orbit, which wasn't many of them.

Not yet, anyway. Trade with *A'Zedi* and the others might change that. And might not. Monsanch was *Unaffiliated*, at least today. Ambassadors and Consuls from various other places, but didn't belong to anyone.

She found the rail station that would take them downtown, close to the hotel where they were staying. Which wasn't the same one that Ambassador Alkes and her staff were in.

Tourists. Mice hiding from view while they had fun and maybe fooled around. Except that she was about as safe as she could get. That was nice, too.

Folks stared openly at Padraig. Tall and dark. Handsome, but so different from the locals. Then they scowled at her, assuming she was a local with some exotic, alien boyfriend.

The first time, she wanted to blush. By the end of the trip, she found herself smiling at people. Daring them to suggest a foreign romp.

Ye gods, this was fun.

She exited the train and followed the signs, comparing them to the map she'd memorized before leaving *Marrakesh*.

Government Plaza was the center, with the main palace directly across from her. Principal Court Building on the same main square, with an Armory on the third side, all three more or less facing a park with a big lake in the middle.

Nice day. Mid-twenties, so she was glad she had a heavier tunic instead of just a shirt.

Zarah let the smells guide her as she walked around. She'd always had something of an iron stomach, with spices others found impossible to eat merely adding zest to her meal. Plus, Padraig had put her in charge.

She ended up at a place with the heavy smell of red sauce lingering. Pastas in various shapes. Sauces in several colors. Flatbread pizzas.

Her stomach rumbled happily and she walked in. They had local currency to spend, and no duty clock going off in six hours for her to shower and prepare for some training certifications.

Vacation.

When was the last time she'd done one of those? Ten years, maybe? She'd been twelve, with her two younger brothers nine and seven. A trip to the coast, and playing in the ocean.

Too many books since then. She settled, then surprised herself by ordering a glass of red wine to go with a baked mess of pasta, red sauce, white cheese, and smells. Padraig got a white sangria and a pizza.

It was almost like a date. When was the last one of those she'd had?

"You're doing fine," Padraig said, so maybe he'd seen the shock and panic in her eyes.

That many years since she'd sat at a table with a guy and nowhere to be.

"I have a question," Zarah replied, keeping her voice low and waiting for him to nod. "How do you maintain a normal life outside of uniform?"

He leaned back and stared over her shoulder.

"It can be easy to simply fall into the job and let it dictate things," Padraig said. "I'm probably more guilty of that than most. Which part did you mean?"

"To an outsider, this probably looks like a date," Zarah muttered carefully. "As intended. I just realized I haven't really had one of those in years."

He nodded sagely. Captainly.

"Jean-Michele didn't like the long separations that came with the navy," he told her. "Nor that I would be more committed to the ship than him. He left, and I haven't really seen anyone since. Almost two years now."

Zarah nodded.

"Same," she offered. "He wanted to think that I'd change into someone who didn't want to go into space. He was wrong."

"They often are," Padraig nodded. "That's the thing that separates us from the rest. That restlessness."

"How do you deal with it?" she asked, figuring that she wouldn't get many opportunities to ask him like this. Or any senior officer. Especially not one who felt old enough to be her dad, even though he wasn't.

"Take what you can get when you can?" he replied. "Chance might be a better person to ask. She has a somewhat normal life, with Robin and the kids. I'm the wanderer."

Zarah considered that. Between the Captain and the First Officer, she supposed that she really did have both ends of a pretty good spectrum to work with, with Stevedore Lynch being more towards Padraig's end, since she'd never married. Nor had kids.

Did she want that for herself? Family? Kids?

Or was the restlessness for her?

Food interrupted before she could get too far down that rabbit hole.

And, across the way, a woman was eyeing her in a way that didn't look right.

10

Padraig caught Zarah's look of concern. And noted where she'd focused as he ate his flatbread. Table in the corner. Woman who had come in after they had, possibly following them, though he hadn't paid that much attention, nor worried that much.

Law enforcement was known to be good in Ilham, and he'd passed several friendly gendarme officers wandering around in the crowd on the way here.

He felt safe.

Zarah, however, was nervous.

He studied his Helm Officer. She'd begun to relax, but it felt like all that had just slid back into a closet somewhere, with her moving to a state of alert, possibly expecting a hostile warship.

"Zarah, we're fine," he reminded her.

Took a moment for her eyes to focus again and turn to him.

He nodded and took a bite.

"People will be watching us," he reminded her quietly. "That's okay."

"Something feels off, Padraig," she replied. "The others were casually interested. She's up to something."

"Noted," he said simply. "I'll hit the head in a moment so I can see her better. You keep eating your casserole."

That seemed to calm her.

Padraig rose after a moment and looked around the entire space to find the hallway to the bathrooms, back next to the kitchen. He put a vacuous smile on his face and started walking that direction.

The woman who had drawn Zarah's attention looked to be approaching middle age. Somewhere close to forty, but not there yet. Maybe five years older than him. Darker than most natives would be, but lighter than him. Idly, he wondered if she were from the *Holy Imperium of Copez*. They tended to that general coloration, with strong classist elements that favored lightness of skin when sorting people socially.

Then you added in a certain level of religious fanaticism that he'd always found off-putting. Even the new Archbishop of Igen, installed six years ago, hadn't really done much other than break the old confederation with *Wronlori* that had underscored the *War of the Third Alliance* and moved them more towards *A'Zedi*. *Traisa* had been exhausted by the previous war, and even eight years later wasn't in a position to help much when *Wronlori* got ambitious again.

And now he was out at Monsanch, trying to do...*something*. For Padraig, it was all still a bit fuzzy, but the Governor had asked him specifically to get involved, so Padraig was here.

The woman watched him go by, but didn't say anything. She was there when he returned, eating and appearing to ignore him.

Not an unattractive woman. Not beautiful, either.

Capable and intent. That was the impression she gave.

He returned to Zarah and went back to eating.

"So far, so good," he murmured to her. "We'll head to the hotel from here and get checked in, then maybe wander around the downtown area some."

"Will she be trouble?" Zarah asked.

"Hard to say," he replied. "We're here, and *Marrakesh* and *A'Zedi* will cause a certain amount of angst and disruption. She might be someone wanting to stay ahead of the chaos. It will be up to her to approach us, though."

"Should I leave you alone some, this afternoon?" Zarah asked, eyes concerned.

"No," he decided. "Let them work for it, whatever *it* is and whoever *they* are."

Padraig went back to his dinner, but he couldn't help but feel that things were in motion.

11

Sana Alkes had gotten Kaitlin to put a couple of her folks from *Marrakesh* down to work on the ground for a few days. Not a vacation, and they weren't spies, but they were operating undercover, and were light-enough skinned to fade into the background.

Thus, she had gotten updates when Boru and Halloran had landed, eaten dinner, and made it to their hotel, a different one than she and her staff were staying at.

She closed the screen with the latest report and rose, checking her look in the mirror by the front door automatically as she approached. And laughing that she'd found two men that her beauty would bounce entirely off of.

Rare, in the diplomatic game, and she supposed that she could still seduce either of them if it really became necessary, but both were friendly at present and even working for her mission.

She opened her door and went down the hotel hallway to the next room, knocking quietly. Alison opened it immediately with an expressive face.

"Time?" Alison asked.

Sana nodded, then stepped back as Alison emerged. Her assistant was as pale as Sana was dark. As tall as Sana was short. As plain as Sana was lush, though she'd never say that. And it wasn't why she'd hired Alison. Most people looked at the woman and didn't realize that they were dealing with a genius-level IQ and a social chameleon.

Her other secret weapon, when Sana could use her own gifts to distract.

Today, Sana was dressed professionally in blue slacks and a blazer, but both cut to emphasize her figure. Alison was in grays that wouldn't draw attention, with a messenger bag slung over one shoulder.

They made their way down to the street and walked. It wasn't far, and the day was gloriously bright and cool overhead. Quickly, they made it to the Governor's palace and got seen through all the layers of security around the man.

Extra heavy still. After the week everyone had had, the armed troopers were keyed up. Rightfully so, but she'd gone ahead and added several minutes slack to her schedule, just in case.

They eventually got to Jamy Hesell. He was even nice and didn't play dominance games by making them wait in a side suite, but instead, had them ushered directly into his office.

It was a nice space. Open and airy. Hesell worked behind a drafting table rather than a desk, and seemed to stand frequently, as it had all manner of mechanical options. The bookshelves on two sides had a wide variety of titles that she caught at a glance, as well as several things she took to be personal trophies.

And a small bowl filled with bits of orange and lemon peel, from the scent they gave off.

Sixth floor, with a fabulous view of the market square below, currently in the process of filling up with an afternoon farmers' market she'd barely avoided in getting here.

He was dressed in a jacket that emphasized how his shoulders appeared to be two meters wide, seemingly tapering down to a point at his belt. It really was a shame he didn't hardly like females, from her own probes and secrets whispered in her ear.

"Welcome, Ambassador," he said, shaking her hand.

Jamy Hesell had strong hands, but not the smooth skin of so many politicians. There was some weekend hobby there that left callouses.

"Thank you, Governor Hesell," she replied. "My assistant, Alison Conagher."

Alison got a handshake, then drew a chair back to a corner where she was out of the way. And memorizing everything. Recordings were lovely, but Alison could add in-depth commentary as she went.

"Thank you for letting me borrow Captain Boru," Hesell began. "I'm not sure he will be successful, but adding an extra player to the game board should help. Hopefully, no harm will come to him."

"I have found Padraig Boru to be highly competent, Governor," Sana replied. "And not just as a command officer. He's young, but I expect him to achieve greater things before he is done. I'm still interested in why you thought that having him poke around might be useful. I know we touched on it earlier, but that was the theoretical, and now we are at the practical, as he is not all that far away, getting settled in."

"We are *Unaffiliated*, Ambassador Alkes," he began, but she cut him off. Politely.

"Please, call me Sana," she said. "If we're somehow co-

conspirators, at least in this little way, we should move past the formal."

"Sana," he nodded, smiling. "And I am Jamy, though most of my staff might swallow their tongues if you called me that in public."

She laughed and nodded.

Their little secret, which made it all the better.

"As I was saying, Monsanch has allies, but nothing formal," Jamy continued. "Consuls and Ambassadors come and go, but Monsanchers would prefer if you kept your wars well away from us."

"Understood, Jamy," she nodded again. "At present, my primary thrust is for trade that might serve to open up this region of space to deeper exploration."

His eyes held a twinkle at her vocabulary, but she maintained innocence. Ripping off all her clothes and throwing herself at the man had been one of the last options on a long and messy list, but she'd moved it even lower after meeting him that first time.

Jamy Hesell wasn't one of those power-hungry politicians who thought with his penis. As so many did.

He paused exactly long enough to make a subtle comment on her language before he smiled, which just showed how smart and adept the man was.

Pity, then.

However, she was prepared for all situations. That came with the job.

"It's a pity that things went so sideways, just as we arrived," she continued before he spoke. "Have your people had any luck tracking the killer of Ambassador Wrezal?"

"They have not," he shook his head. "And the scope of the party's invite list did little to cull the suspects down, as he was known to have slept with nearly half of them at one time or another."

"Open minded?" she asked, following up other rumors.

"Voraciously omnisexual, Sana," Jamy laughed. "Perhaps aggressively so. Still, all consenting adults, so nothing that rose to the level of official concern."

"Were you and he ever...?" she let it trail off rather than finish.

"We were not," Jamy replied. "As Governor, there are certain boundaries that must be observed around officially accredited foreigners."

Sana nodded. Not many politicians were good about that sort of thing either, opening themselves up to any and all manner of blackmail.

"Hmmmm," she grunted to herself.

"Yes?" Jamy asked.

"I had the thought of blackmail, however unrelated," Sana offered delicately. "If he had that many lovers, did he also have enemies who might have chosen now to strike? Was he perhaps holding some Damoclean sword over someone's head and they saw an opportunity at retribution?"

Jamy shrugged.

"It would be something of an understatement to call the whole a swampy morass," he replied. "That was why I was hoping that Captain Boru might approach it sideways, thereby jarring someone into revealing themselves, while I have my entire establishment ready to land on them like a ton of bricks."

Sana nodded. Complicated games. Normally, a simple ship's captain would be entirely lost, to be dropped into such a situation.

Sana knew better. She'd read deeply on the man when her

superiors had suggested him and *Marrakesh* for this mission. And met and worked closely with both Boru and Lynch, and all of their people.

To call him merely highly competent was to underestimate the man.

Padraig Boru was *dangerously* so.

But only to the enemy.

"Agreed, Jamy," she said. "For now, let us meander aimlessly onto the dry topic of tariffs and inspection protocols..."

12

Padraig had adjusted his personal clock to local time already, so the approaching evening filled him with energy, rather than dragging. Captains were never off duty, even when they were asleep.

He held ultimate power. And the final responsibility when something went wrong.

That was why he worked so hard to get his officers trained up right. Chance Messier could handle things for a few days while he was down here, but it was still his head on the chopping block if something went wrong up there.

He would deal with it.

For now, they had checked into the hotel. Then had a bit of downtime to relax and for that farmers market to wind itself up. Not quite a night market, as many worlds and cultures might do it, but close enough.

Now, people. Noise. Smells. Music and fried food wafting over the crowd as he walked with Zarah. All of their gear was in the room, save for a few things tucked into inner pockets where a thief couldn't easily dislodge them.

Safe enough, with many police officers walking around as well.

The assassination had caused them to hype up some, even as the rest of the crowd seemed to be looking for an emotional release. Possibly a busy week and they wanted to weekend it?

He didn't know. It was enough that he and Zarah could walk and enjoy themselves.

Still, Padraig felt eyes on him. And not just folks surprised at seeing someone dark from *A'Zedi* walking around, as there were a few folks of a similarly walnut or ochre coloration, though not many.

All of humanity was a spectrum, ranging from the pale or burnished golden skin most common in *Traisa* through the darkest bronzes of *A'Zedi*, with genetics throwing up all manner of combinations every generation.

Some of the eyes didn't feel friendly, but not in a racist way. Watching.

He could take care of himself. And Zarah was tougher than she gave herself credit for.

They threaded the crowd, looking at tables with trinkets or various foodstuffs, but weren't really shopping.

Being seen.

A woman appeared at the edge of his vision.

She'd been in the restaurant earlier. Watching them. Watching him.

Padraig acknowledged her with an empty nod as they made eye contact. Two strangers in a crowd.

Music would make conversation complicated, as someone had a drum solo with a lot of enthusiasm over there, driving a singer to great emotional heights, though the sound system wasn't really doing her any favors when it came to clarity.

Raw noise he felt in his sternum.

Padraig touched Zarah's arm, but she'd already seen the woman as well.

Zarah leaned close.

"Should I wander off a bit?" she asked, mouth touching his ear.

Padraig considered it. Now might be as good a time as any, if someone wanted to take his measure.

"Not far," he replied, turning to let her read his lips.

Nearby, the song ended and it was like someone had thrown open the shades to let light in. He hadn't realized how heavy the sound had been leaning on his shoulders.

Zarah moved down a side corridor in the tables, while he turned and continued straight ahead.

There was a table that caught his eye for standing out so much from the others. Instead of jars of food or jewelry, the woman behind the table seemed to be selling books. Actual paper printed with ink. Some lurid mystery from the cover and the title.

Padraig had a few such relics, but most of the time he was working with reports, either from Chance or things he needed to send on to command.

He couldn't remember the last time he'd sat down and read fiction for pleasure.

Still, it let him come to rest. In the open. With witnesses.

And the band must be done, because quieter music started up next. Something soothing and backgroundy, after whatever raucous performance he'd missed over there.

Not that he minded.

That woman was still there when he glanced over. Maintaining a discreet distance, as it were.

Padraig ignored her for now and focused on the woman

selling actual books. Older. Homely in a plain way. Somewhat overweight, but not bad.

Unhealthy, that was it. He was used to military officers and crew who had quarterly fitness requirements and fierce competition for promotion, so they were all constantly working out and training.

This was a civilian with an entirely different lifestyle. On a new world and an alien culture.

"Good morning, sir," she said brightly.

"Morning?" Padraig asked, glancing up at the setting sun.

"It is an ancient concept," she smiled. "The first time you see someone, your joint day begins, so it is morning."

Didn't make any sense, but she had conviction. He could honor that.

Padraig picked up one of the books. Heavy, when he was used to a reader a third as thick and smaller in all dimensions. He flipped it over and read the back.

Mystery. A crime had occurred, and someone had hired a civilian specialist to solve it, when the authorities couldn't. Or wouldn't.

That struck a little too close to home for Padraig, at least on certain levels.

Still, it intrigued him as well, so he flipped it over and opened it to read the first page.

Not bad. Gripping, though he wasn't sure he understood all the context.

Enough to catch his attention.

Padraig looked up at the woman's expectant smile. He checked the price and dug into his pocket for local cash.

"Would you like it signed?" she asked.

It registered on Padraig that she was the author, rather than merely a shopkeeper, as she had a dozen different titles in front of her with the same name.

Huh.

"Please," he nodded, watching her sign it, then pull out a small bag from under the table and put it in as he gave her money.

"Thank you," Padraig said, turning to go.

The other woman hadn't wandered off. Zarah hadn't gone far, but he found himself almost alone.

But for several thousand other people shopping.

He moved towards the stranger from the restaurant.

Perhaps it was time to push things a bit.

13

Padraig stared at the woman as she stared back, sailing right up like two shuttles preparing to dock as he approached her.

He came to rest directly in front of her, an expectant smile on his lips and a hard seriousness in his eyes.

And waited.

She wasn't as flustered as an innocent would be right now. Nor did she look around for an assistant about to box him in.

He waited.

It was a somewhat rude thing to do, throwing silence in someone's face. But he had known it to work in the past.

"Captain Boru," she acknowledged. "My name is Skye Bancroft."

So she knew who he was. And had been watching.

Who else around here was watching him?

Or her.

"Madame Bancroft," he nodded. "How may I be of assistance?"

After all, his activities were supposedly a closely kept secret.

Nobody outside the Governor's palace should know he was here. Especially this quickly.

As with the mission to Albany, and that terrible Leviathan *Sundering Wrath*, he assumed a leak of information into the hands of folks not supposed to know.

Spies, as it were, when he was, as the character in the book by his side, an outsider without all that training.

"My organization wished to contact you *sub rosa*, sir," Bancroft replied. "Unofficially, at least on the surface."

"I see," he nodded, moving that last half step forward that intruded on her personal space in most cultures.

They weren't dancing, but only because they weren't touching. Or moving.

She didn't step back, holding her ground at his intrusion.

"And your organization is?" he asked quietly, smelling the breath mint she'd had after dinner. Wintergreen, with a hint of citrus underneath.

"The *Holy Imperium*," she replied in a whisper, leaning in a bit.

Padraig wondered what she thought of his aftershave. He hadn't picked it to seduce a woman, but supposed that it might work for that, too.

"And the need for secrecy?" he asked.

"Monsanch is a complicated place, Captain," she said, practically breathing in his ear.

He wondered if they'd thought to send a woman to seduce him.

Much, much harder, even in normal circumstances.

Still, it would make a useful cover.

"Should we go someplace private to chat?" he said, turning his head to the point that their cheeks touched.

"What about your friend?" Bancroft asked.

"Should she accompany us?" he breathed.

It almost sounded like they had missed a vital piece of the puzzle. That whoever she represented had thought he had a local in tow, rather than his Helm Officer in civilian clothing.

How could he use that to his advantage?

"The Bishop would prefer privacy, if possible, Captain," she replied, one hand on his elbow now.

Padraig knew where the Embassy Cathedral was located. Several blocks back from the square itself and not all that impressive as a building, as the *Holy Imperium* had never had much success proselytizing in this region of space.

The culture of *Copez* was more of a relic of older eras, though the current *Holy Imperium* had managed to transform itself into an interstellar nation with a certain level of militancy, closer to the rim.

Padraig leaned back enough to look Bancroft in the eyes. Earnest enough, it seemed, though looks could be deceiving.

"Should I approach the embassy by the front door or a side?" he asked. "Where should I find you after I speak with my friend?"

"I will take the north avenue," she sighed. "And meet you a block from here, if that's acceptable?"

"It is," Padraig nodded, adding a smile. "Shortly."

He turned away and located Zarah in the press, moving her direction without any alarm.

She was shopping for jewelry, to the casual eye, though her attention was quietly focused his way.

"Good news?" she asked as he slid up next to her, pretending to study a set of handmade charms to hang from a necklace.

"A contact from *Copez*," he replied under his breath. "You

return to the hotel with my book, and I will check in with you in no more than two hours."

"Should I sound an alarm at that point?" Zarah asked.

"Call the governor first, then Chance," Padraig decided.

"Understood, sir," she said.

He handed her the bag with the mystery novel and squared his shoulders.

What had he gotten himself into?

14

Chance looked up as someone rapped on the hatch to the day office. With Padraig and Zarah on the ground, she'd shifted to standing longer watches herself, as well as making sure folks like Andrea Whelan, *Marrakesh*'s Coxswain herself, did a lot of extra training for younger crew and officers.

Padraig firmly believed that any officer should be able to work with any enlisted crew member to solve whatever problems came up, including taking command of the ship if they had to.

They weren't there yet, but she was spending time in the office instead of on the bridge to reinforce that lesson. Working close by to let them handle it, but close while they were in charge if something came up.

She reached out and tapped the button to slide the hatch open, revealing Nyssa Taggart standing there, while Andrea was seated in Padraig's chair behind her, with a grin like a juvenile delinquent on her face.

"Come," Chance told Nyssa, nodding to the Coxswain.

Nyssa took the closer seat and fidgeted.

No better word for it. Couldn't sit still. Eyes wandered instead of making contact. Hands clenched and unclenched.

"So talk," Chance told the young woman.

Nyssa paled, then focused. Drew a hard breath deep as Chance watched. Came to rest, at least briefly.

"Captain Boru tasked me with studying the cryptographic data available, sir," Nyssa began.

Chance nodded. She'd talked it over with him extensively before he'd left.

"Current status?" Chance asked, prodding the woman.

"I might have accidentally cracked somebody's code, sir," Nyssa replied.

Chance let her eyes speak volumes in size. She hadn't worked all that closely with Taggart, but Padraig had let her know how sharp he thought the young woman was.

He'd even suggested that she would be commanding her own cruiser in another twenty years, if things worked out. Chance leaned forward to listen, chin resting on her hands.

"Whose?" she asked with an inviting smile.

"It's a *Traisa* code, sir," Nyssa replied. "A message to the Enlightened Tyrant himself, but someone sent it in the clear first, then turned around and sent it encoded an hour later. Nav computer looked at the hash of the second message and extrapolated a match to the first."

"And you've confirmed this?" Chance pressed, gasping a little at the potential for mischief.

Traisa was an ally in this latest conflict, but not all that involved.

Wronlori had declared war on *A'Zedi* and *Copez* this time around, and focused most of their efforts there, since the *Enlightened Tyranny* was still exhausted from the last war. Able to hold their own lines, but not a threat to attack a *Wronlori* fleet or world with any seriousness.

Nyssa had gone a little pale.

"I was able to go back and read three-quarters of the messages that they've sent via aetherial comms since we arrived," Nyssa said quietly. "Once I knew what the code looked like, that is."

Chance leaned back and considered the implications.

"Anything bad?" she asked her Radio Officer.

Nyssa squirmed.

"Nyssa?"

"I can't be sure, sir," Nyssa admitted. "One message simply read *It's done* without any other signifiers or signatures. The timing was questionable, as that message went out ninety-four minutes after the assassination was discovered, according to the timeline provided by the Stevedore. The first, uncoded message went out two hours after that."

Chance bit her tongue rather than reply. Nyssa was correct in her suspicion that it might have been an inside job, but all the details Chance had read over the last several days merely extended the list of people who might want Joshua Wrezal dead for a variety of reasons. Not a scumball who desperately deserved it, but certainly a man with a variety of underworld connections, as well as an impressive string of current and ex-lovers.

Nothing narrowed it down to the one person who might have held the Adjustable Disruptor that had actually killed him, fired with a narrow beam at short range.

And if Wrezal had seen it coming, he ought to have been able to yell or something, so Chance assumed that he'd been surprised.

Plus, dressed at the time, when she'd heard a few rumors

from Sana Alkes that finding the man nude and *in flagrante delicto*, as it were, wouldn't have been at all that surprising, or out of character.

Nyssa was waiting on pins and needles, watching.

"You've done excellent work, Nyssa," Chance replied, watching the young woman relax. "Bundle it all up for me to review, then see if you can crack someone else."

"Sir?"

"If the *Traisa* embassy sent that message to the Enlightened Tyrant, did someone else copy it and send it home themselves?" Chance asked. "If you can get a hash match once, that suggests that maybe you could get a second, once you knew what to look for."

"Oh," Nyssa uttered, surprised. Then her eyes brightened and focused. "OH! I'll see what I can do, sir."

Chance nodded as the young woman rose, smiling to put her at ease.

If they could read messages other folks sent, at least until someone updated all of their codes, what could *Marrakesh* learn out here?

Once she was alone, Chance let the weight of the discovery settle as well.

If Nyssa could do it, could others? And had anyone been able to crack *Marrakesh*'s codes on messages sent to the fleet? Chance expected some of the other messages to trigger a raft of responses, though she rated it low that someone would send another warship to Monsanch on short notice.

More likely was that *Traisa* might send a replacement ambassador on a priority transport, one of those small, fast yachts that could reach Mark Eleven speeds. Eleven light-years per hour, when *Marrakesh* had been able to claw her way up to Six Point *Two* while fleeing that Leviathan, and that had been a surprise to everyone involved, though it had proven to be the thing that kept them alive.

Wouldn't take Supreme Autocrat Arodd Torray long to send someone to replace Wrezal if he was in a hurry.

Especially if they'd planned for it.

What would that tell her?

15

Padraig had separated from Zarah, then made his way to where the barriers kept ground traffic out of the square as other pedestrians came and went.

He got a block north before he saw Bancroft emerge from an alcove to a business that had closed for the day. Padraig hadn't paid that close of attention either time he'd seen her before, beyond noting that she was a fairly attractive woman in her late thirties.

She wore a skirt and matching ruana in a mist green, with burgundy edging and pattern painted on. Made her look tall and slender, but she was shorter than Zarah, even with a bit of a heel on her black leather lace-ups.

She still gave off the impression of a hawk, resting on a perch and waiting for the hunt to begin.

Padraig hoped that he wasn't intended as her prey tonight.

Bancroft reinforced that image when she stepped close and hooked her arm about his.

"Captain," she smiled.

"Padraig," he corrected her. "I'm off duty."

Make of that what you will.

"And I am Skye," she said, bobbing her head as they fell into rhythm walking. "Thank you for joining me."

"I wished to see more of Ilham, Skye," Padraig replied. "The prettier parts."

She blushed and bobbed her head again, like a nervous tic, then fell silent.

He wasn't lying, as she was attractive enough. Not remotely his tastes, but he wasn't about to insult the bishop if the man was going to all this effort to talk to him without simply sending a messenger to his hotel.

Obviously, they wanted things quieter.

Her heels clicked on the cobblestones that had been set down to make this sidewalk, when Padraig was used to metal decks that rang hollowly, or concrete that thumped. He walked silently next to her as they brushed through the thinner crowd here as folks either headed out for a night on the town or home for an early alarm.

Street lights kept things bright enough for people, and the crowd was still reasonably thick, but they made good time. Over and down, running along the long flank of the cathedral itself at one point.

Granite, from the looks of it. Yellowy sand colored, cut into squares a meter on a side and with the surface left bulging out and rough. Three stories, running about half of the block, with what looked to be more modern buildings attached beyond that. Perhaps the cathedral had expanded? Or were these offices for folks not directly involved with the Church's business?

Padraig hadn't ever really paid that much attention to *Copez*, save to note that the *Holy Imperium* tended to build compact warships that were like angry bulldogs whenever they went into combat, as opposed to the sleek greyhounds of *Wronlori*.

Skye led him to an alcove in the gap between cathedral and wood buildings, where a brick wall connected the two and kept out random pedestrians. She moved quickly and placed her hand on a sensor set at shoulder level, where someone would be unlikely to brush it.

The device lit up and scanned her hand. A moment later, the door clicked solidly.

Skye pushed it open, drawing him after her with her other hand.

Padraig wasn't immediately keyed up for violence, but he also moved a bit slow into the opening, looking around before letting himself be trapped inside.

It was a grass-covered courtyard inside, planted with bushes in places and two trees that stretched out and provided a canopy overhead. He didn't know the species, but trees weren't his thing. They would provide shade on a hot day, while lights at shoulder level illuminated the place now.

Skye moved towards the back of the cathedral building, rather than the things that looked more like offices, now holding his left hand in her right as they walked. A saunter, as it were.

She approached a rear door and again used a hand scanner to unlock it.

Inside, the hallway revealed had a foreboding air. Not enough lights, and those tuned towards a more golden-red range than the pure white he was used to on a starship. Stone floors underfoot instead of metal decks, interrupted by rugs that ran down the center with a half-meter gap along both walls.

Niches and pedestals held art objects: busts, jewelry, and

small paintings. Larger portraits of various men in the robes of the Imperium lined the walls every four meters or so.

Padraig hadn't seen anyone since they left the streets.

Skye led him to a staircase up, still clicking as she walked, while he concentrated on moving quietly.

And memorizing his path, in case he needed to escape later.

She did not pause at the second floor, but took him up to the third, then the fourth, emerging to a door on a small landing. She knocked. A man in dark gray clothing opened it, studying both of them.

He had the air of a bodyguard, hyperalert like a hound smelling trouble, though Padraig was an invited guest.

At least he hoped so.

The man stepped back silently, nodding them in. Skye drew Padraig in, then the door closed behind him.

While the downstairs parts Padraig had seen had been quiet and not particularly ostentatious, this room made up for it.

There was a man seated at the far end of the room in a chair Padraig could only qualify as a throne. Dark-stained wood, etched and inlaid with gems and gold. More gold on the walls behind him, as well as silk hangings in a variety of colors that almost gave the room the feel of being inside a tent somewhere.

A sliding glass door was closed, but revealed a small patio beyond, presumably with a view of the city. Or perhaps a nearby park.

Skye drew him towards the man, so Padraig studied this bishop.

He wore the robes, in green. As Padraig approached, he stood. Short and portly. Not quite fat, but not a threat to run down even a lame mule. Bald, with a port-wine-stain birthmark on the top of his forehead and ranging back, in such a way that it might have been invisible until he started losing his hair in his twenties.

Probably forty years ago, from the wrinkles on his face.

Skye drew him close.

"Your Eminence, allow me to present Captain Boru of the *A'Zedi* cruiser *Marrakesh*," she began. "Captain Boru, this is Bishop Murphy, the *Holy Imperium*'s Ambassador to Monsanch."

"Captain Boru," the bishop extended a hand. "Welcome."

Padraig wondered if the man expected him to kiss it, like the *Holy Imperium of Copez* practiced internally. He shook it instead, gripping but not squeezing.

At the ill-fated party, Padraig had merely stood in the background as Sana Alkes had been introduced to the bishop, attention largely elsewhere as he'd originally planned on being here only a few weeks at most, delivering a new embassy before withdrawing for his next mission.

He wondered how soon he might escape the current situation.

"Sir," Padraig said precisely.

He was out of uniform. Supposedly undercover, but certainly someone knew where he was and how to find him, when that should have been a secret.

None of this was official business, so he could play it like a civilian. If he remembered what it was like to be one. That had been more than twenty years ago.

"Please, sit." The bishop gestured Padraig to a nearby chair that wasn't nearly as pretty as the man's throne.

Or as tall.

Still, he did. Comfortable-enough chair. Skye moved to a side table and filled two glasses with a red wine, returning and handing them out.

Padraig took a sip and noted that the bishop liked those big, chewy cabernets that had always struck him like paint thinner mixed with a hint of rancid grapefruit juice underneath.

He could sip it, though. Guest, and all that.

"I wanted a chance to chat with you before you began poking and prodding at some of the less seemly bits of Monsanch culture, Captain," Bishop Murphy began, revealing just how deep the man's spies must be in Governor Hesell's staff.

Were there any secrets on Monsanch?

"At present, I've only barely landed, sir," Padraig replied with a neutral smile. "Had an early dinner, then began to learn a bit about Ilham itself. What parts should I be worried about?"

There, let him fill in some blanks, with whatever ax the man had to grind. Hadn't that been Hesell's term? Grinding axes?

"Joshua Wrezal was a complicated figure, Captain," Murphy replied. "A man of immense appetites and almost a sybarite when it came to enjoying himself in this life."

Padraig refrained from commenting, given the richness of the furniture, art, and even clothing on the man in front of him. Also, Bishop Murphy didn't look like a man who had missed many meals recently. Or ever.

"What did he do to make such an enemy, do you suppose?" Padraig asked innocently. "After all, someone saw the need to execute the man with a pistol in the midst of the governor's reception."

Murphy shrugged in an eloquent way that suggested he might have a six-page list of infractions to accuse Wrezal of committing. Or admitting.

Governor Hesell had sent Padraig a briefing packet, seemingly culled from his own espionage and security forces, listing known and suspected lovers, business partners, and underworld contacts.

Everyone in Ilham had been in bed with the man at one point, literally or figuratively, it seemed. Or both.

"It could have been anyone," Murphy nodded sagely. "I would concentrate on his criminal contacts, were I in your shoes."

Padraig nodded, wondering if the man was attempting to sell him a pig in a poke. Or deflect an investigation from looking into various connections to the bishop and his establishment?

"Do you perhaps have a few names I might inquire against?" Padraig pressed, wondering who the man might want to implicate.

It all felt a shade heavy handed. As if the Bishop of Monsanch had secrets and needed to make sure that Padraig didn't accidentally uncover them.

Not that it should matter all that much. Monsanch was a vast distance from the *Holy Imperium*'s capital at Igen, physically as well as culturally. Still, he smiled and considered guilty consciences.

Murphy turned to Skye Bancroft and some unspoken message was conveyed. Padraig wondered if she would be providing him such a list. Perhaps under the cover of them being lovers?

He knew that many such assignations occurred, perhaps not as luridly as spy videos portrayed them, but he assumed a kernel of truth there.

"What about *Wronlori*?" Padraig turned the tables sideways now.

"What about them?" Murphy asked, taken aback from the quick surprise on his face, already receding.

"It strikes me that *A'Zedi* and *Copez* are currently at war with *Wronlori*," Padraig reminded the man. "The *Enlightened Tyranny of Traisa* is allied with us, though not directly fighting. Would *Wronlori* gain from assassinating the *Traisa* ambassador?"

"Ah, of course," Murphy nodded a moment later. "Captain, the wars of the rim do not impact us, so much, this close to the galactic core. I would wager that your *Marrakesh* was only allowed to transport Sana Alkes to Monsanch specifically because it is a transport, and not a line warship. All four major governments have a gentleman's agreement to not send such vessels to the colonies of the interior."

"I see," Padraig replied evenly

On the surface, it made perfect sense. *Marrakesh* was a Tactical Transport. Not a cruiser, though built on the same hull. If such an agreement had been made, it also explained the lack of other warships around, when there were so many large freighters moving about.

He would have to figure a way to send a message back to headquarters to confirm. Or not.

Did it matter? He wasn't sure.

"And thus, there is no need to kill an enemy ambassador, because they aren't really the enemy here?" Padraig guessed.

"Exactly," Murphy beamed. "I'm so glad you are sharp enough to grasp that. My great concern has been that Jamy was all set to cause trouble around here by unleashing a military man who really didn't grasp the finer points of the sorts of diplomacy we perform, here in the interior."

Padraig bowed his head in acknowledgment. He supposed that most naval officers might have come in like bulls in china shops. Especially given the sorts of latitude that Jamy Hesell had given him.

Not exactly a blank page, but not far short of it.

He considered his options. His nigh-unlimited options, though no doubt Murphy and Bancroft would be seeking to channel his energies in ways that perhaps showed them in the best light. Or concealed things they weren't prepared to explain to a journalist or their own government.

"In that case, could I prevail upon you for a quiet invitation to call upon the *Wronlori* ambassador?" Padraig smiled, watching Murphy's face freeze perfectly solid for a moment. "I was unable to meet her at that first reception, as Sana Alkes had planned a quiet, private meeting later, obviously unaware of how things are done around here."

He held himself perfectly innocent as he watched Murphy go through what looked like the stages of death before the man finally acquiesced. Again, the sharp look at Skye Bancroft to convey something.

Padraig wondered if he should simply present himself at the door to the *Wronlori* embassy, first thing tomorrow morning.

Foxes. Hen houses.

That would be rude. Still, how often would he ever get a chance to meet someone from the *United Technocracy* in such relaxed circumstances as Bishop Murphy suggested? Last time, it had been a duel to the death with *Sundering Wrath*.

Was it possible to talk to *Wronlori* like civilized adults?

Padraig had his doubts, but he didn't have to negotiate an end to the war, either.

"You have given me much to contemplate," Murphy said in such a way that Padraig recognized a dismissal. "We shall be up late, organizing things for you, Captain."

He rose and bowed politely.

"And you as well, sir," Padraig replied. "It has certainly opened my eyes, and hopefully I will be able to negotiate the situation with the subtlety that will do you justice."

Again, a flash of something, but it was gone too quickly for Padraig to classify it.

Still, dangerous waters concealed under a quiet surface.

He would have to watch his back.

Skye Bancroft smiled and took his arm again as he turned to the door.

16

Padraig quietly let go a deep breath as he got out of the main cathedral building and at least as far as the shaded courtyard. Skye Bancroft still held his arm, like two lovers on a promenade, but he wasn't fooled. Bishop Murphy treated her like some sort of spy, and he'd spent too much time around such folks after the recent events at Albany, when Kaitlin and Chance had uncovered and captured such a man hiding in Dr. Borsheva's team.

At the same time, Padraig presumed that most officers like him had never spent that much time around folks working in the shadows like her to understand anything concealed about her. It wasn't a military thing.

He let her lead him to the exit, wondering how far this mission of hers would take him. And how far he would let it go.

Internally, he laughed at the thought that Zarah provided an excuse for him to avoid any propositions from Bancroft. At least for tonight.

Just how open minded were folks around here? Granted, he'd only met the Governor, but Bishop Murphy felt more like a throwback to a more genial and corrupt civilization, which was rather how Padraig tended to see the *Holy Imperium* most of the time anyway.

Monsanchers felt more like that band of hardy pioneers still dedicated to building up a society of rugged individualism, rather than...what was the term Murphy had used?

Sybarites.

Sounded more like a damning indictment of an ambassador from the rim. Or perhaps several?

What games did people like that play, separated so far from their home cultures?

They reached the exit and paused. Bancroft turned inward to face him without letting go of his arm, until they were almost dancing again.

"I will need to spend time gathering intelligence data for you, Padraig," she said, almost wistfully. As if she'd rather return to his hotel with him.

"Should we plan for a lunch or dinner?" he countered. "And how quickly?"

"Dinner tomorrow," she nodded sharply. "I can have everything prepared by then, and will call on you at your hotel in the fourth hour."

He nodded, still watching her. Skye reminded him of a hawk, even now.

She leaned forward expectantly, so Padraig joined her for a quick kiss. Nothing passionate. Hardly more than one might greet a stranger when traveling to Jakra.

She smiled knowingly.

"Until tomorrow," she smiled.

He nodded and watched her open the door that let him escape. Rude way to frame it, even in his own head, but not entirely wrong.

Not much time had passed in this outside world, for all that he felt like that one man in the fairy tale that had fallen asleep for five hundred years. Folks were still coming and going, though these streets weren't as busy as the main thoroughfare.

Padraig made his way back to busier streets, then headed towards his hotel, uncaring if he was being followed at this point.

What was the need to hide, if Bishop Murphy's organization had already read his instructions from Hesell? Who else might want to chat?

Fortunately, he made it back safely.

A knock on Zarah's door and it opened quickly. She stepped back and gestured him in.

Padraig paused and looked both ways before entering, wondering if someone might assume things not happening.

She closed it and he moved to a chair in the corner, gesturing her to sit on the bed across from him.

"Everything okay?" she asked when he didn't speak immediately.

"I had a meeting with the bishop," he began, quickly recounting the conversation for her, along with his misgivings and various far-fetched ideas that had come up on the walk home.

Zarah paused, face scrunched up in deep thought.

"I like that term," she nodded, still serious. "Sybarite. They don't get us at all, do they?"

"You mean the navy?" he asked, brightening. She nodded. "You are correct. They do not. To them, everything seems to be one long cocktail party and social affair. I wonder if Hesell is managing to play them all off against one another that way."

"Makes sense," Zarah replied. "We're a different culture entirely, though as captain you seem able to change hats as you need."

"Long practice," he nodded. "Plus too much time after Albany, talking to those sorts of folks. But yes, we think differently."

"So she's going to throw herself at you tomorrow?" Zarah asked with a grin.

"Something," Padraig grumbled. "You should be concerned that she might want you along."

Zarah's face suddenly looked like she'd sucked a lemon dry, so he grinned at her.

"What's this?" Padraig said, suddenly realizing that he had a piece of paper tucked into a pocket that he didn't remember from before.

He pulled it out and studied it. About the size of his palm, folded four times. There was a time written in the local clock for fairly early in the morning, along with the name of the hotel's restaurant. And some sort of image, hand-sketched. A disk, or rather, half of one, with the edge broken raggedly, as though into two pieces.

He didn't remember anything like this from before, but he'd also had to walk through crowds both times. It was possible that someone had slipped it into his pocket while bumping him. That had happened enough times.

"Recognition code?" Zarah asked, standing closer now to look at it.

"Looks like," Padraig nodded.

"How do you want to handle it?" she asked.

"We'll both be down there for breakfast," he said. "They can show up and join us, if they dare."

"In the light of day?" she turned serious.

"It feels like too much of Monsanch's business would likely benefit from such a thing," Padraig replied.

He rose and made his way to the door.

Tomorrow morning was going to be here far too early.

17

Chance got on the line quickly when Padraig called to send them an update.

"Nyssa has had some successes with the job you gave her," Chance told him at the top. "I've tasked her with extending it as far as she can."

Silence. Padraig digesting.

"Are our communications secure?" he asked a moment later.

"I hope so," Chance replied. "However..."

"Understood," Padraig said. "See what you can do there, given the limitations of operating in the field."

"I've had some thoughts along those lines, but that might require sending down a new set of personal transmitters for you and Zarah," she told him.

"Do that as soon as Nyssa thinks she's good to go," she heard him order. "We can always keep hopping forward as we need. I don't know if anyone else has something like a nav computer handy, short of the governor himself, without any other ships. Or someone as smart as Nyssa."

"Are you expecting any?" she pressed.

"No, save for a fast transport at most," he said.

Chance listened to a rapid rundown of his conversation with the bishop, as well as notes towards a meeting of some sort in the morning.

"Should you have a security detail with you?" Chance asked when he finished.

"I think that would be exactly wrong, in spite of my cover apparently being blown all to hell even before things got started," he replied. "Zarah has a comm. Maybe you should send down a pair of Type Three Personal Disruptors with the same package that has updated comms. I'd feel more comfortable with something like that tucked into my pocket. Or concealed in my hand as I walked into some of these meetings."

"Understood, Padraig," Chance acknowledged. "Anything else?"

"No, I plan to lock the door and sleep as soon as I'm done with you," he said.

"Check in when you wake up," Chance ordered. "I'll have updates."

"Will do."

The line went dead and Chance considered her options. *Marrakesh* had been reset to local time in the capital below, so it was late in everybody's day.

At the same time, starships never slept.

She keyed a line aft.

"Engineering. Garber."

"Chief, I need someone to maybe stay up all night helping Squire Taggart reprogram the encryption on a pair of personal transmitters, for delivery to the Captain as soon as we can get them to the ground," Chance began. "Who's the best person to work on that?"

"Maybe me, Commander," he replied. "Unless you want me to wake up the Cox'n for it."

"You'll do, Garber," Chance said. "Find me three pairs and make sure one pair is ready to go as soon as possible. The other two pairs will go down at some point in the future. I'll send Taggart aft shortly, so have the wardroom brew you up a batch of coffee. Also, have an armorer check out a pair of Type Threes to accompany the transmitters in a diplomatic pouch."

"On it, sir," Garber said.

Chance switched lines. This one beeped a couple of times.

"Taggart," Nyssa came on the line, bleary from waking out of a deep sleep.

Couldn't be helped.

"Nyssa, I just talked to Captain Boru, down on the surface," Chance said. "I need you to head aft and work with Carpenter Garber on encrypting the first of several sets of personal transmitters for physical delivery. Obviously, we don't want to send down a code update that someone else might intercept. I'd also like them down on the surface come morning in the capital."

"Understood, sir," Nyssa replied, waking quickly. "In motion now."

Chance cut the line and leaned back.

What was it Padraig had said? A fox in the henhouse?

Interesting image, but she kept wondering if he was really a stalking horse for someone else.

18

Nyssa blinked rapidly to wake herself up as she went down the main starboard corridor to Engineering. *Marrakesh* had two such hallways, running down the outside instead of the center because of the modules that got plugged in.

Late in the ship's day. Not many people about as she traversed corridors. She'd stopped by the wardroom for a mug of coffee to help shake the sleep from her mind. It made perfect sense to send down updated comms, after what she'd managed to do to break a diplomatic code of *Traisa*.

At the same time, she wondered if the First Officer was overreacting.

Or underreacting.

Nyssa wasn't sure as she went through the primary airlock separating Engineering from the rest of the ship, extremely secured and reinforced bulkheads designed to channel any explosion outwards rather than letting it flash inward and potentially gut the ship.

Garber was standing inside when she arrived. Ship's Carpenter, or senior enlisted man in the Engineering section.

She hadn't worked with the man all that much prior, so she didn't know him that well.

Big. Taller than even Captain Boru, and still managing to feel stocky. Starting to go gray on top, though he still had a thick head of hair, almost a mane as she looked at it. Probably needed to get a haircut, but that might just be her own proclivities.

She'd keep her head perfectly shaved and polished if the Captain would allow it.

"Squire," he nodded as she came to rest. "I've set us up in Workroom A if you're okay with that?"

Nyssa smiled and nodded. Roderic Garber wasn't much younger than her dad, so it felt weird for him to be deferring to her. At the same time, those silly folks had gone ahead and made her an officer, however foolish she occasionally thought such an action was.

Garber turned and walked that direction rapidly, long legs moving in almost a blur. She moved in his wake.

Two personal transmitters had been placed on a work cloth, with several different tool boxes handy, from something a jeweler might use all the way up to wrenches for a plasma conduit.

Nyssa started to say something, then held her tongue. He had no idea what she might need, and had gone ahead and had tried to place everything at her fingertips.

Thinking ahead. Planning ahead.

There was a lesson there she suddenly understood better than she had even as recently as going to bed.

She took the nearer chair and set her mug down next to a sealed carafe of more, as she needed it. Garber's mug was nearby. He took the other chair, eyeing her expectantly.

Time to officer.

Nyssa took a breath and tried not to think about lecturing her dad about things. However close to the truth it might be.

"We're not going to incorporate a permanently modified encryption chip," she began, waiting for him to nod. He'd gotten her all the gear to do just that. "Instead, I want to take one of our standard chips and directly flash it with a new code we're going to generate now. I'll need a Diagnostic Probe to begin."

He reached across the table and grabbed one, putting it directly into her hands.

Engineering tool. These folks lived by them, frequently carrying a short-range version in one pocket and possibly even sleeping with it under their pillow. She didn't ask.

The standard Probe was fifteen centimeters wide by twenty tall, and about a centimeter and a half thick. Screen for displaying information. They came with a variety of built-in sensors and scanners you could point at something to do things with.

Nyssa had never really gone all that deep into the capabilities of such a device, but she supposed that she'd need to learn about them if she wanted to leave the ship on adventures like Zarah was having right now.

Did she want to?

She wasn't sure. Didn't need to know today.

"You pull the data cards from both," she said as she worked. "I'm going to go ahead and have the ship's computer generate me a code that should be strong enough for a week on the ground."

He nodded and she got to work. The Diagnostic Probe was already linked to the main computer. She logged it fully into the nav system and typed a series of commands she had prepared earlier against Commander Messier giving her this order today.

Didn't take long, but that was having so much raw processing power handy to do the job. Hopefully, nobody would be able to reverse engineer her work later, but she'd deal with that by making it more complicated next time she had to do this.

And maybe spending a little time studying this sort of thing with an eye towards a new certification. There were dozens she could go after, but Advanced Cryptography hadn't been one she'd ever expected to need.

What else did an adventurer officer need, if she was going to make this a career? Maybe she'd talk to the Captain about it when he got back.

"Ready?" she asked.

Garber put a chip in her palm with a serious nod. Nyssa slipped it into the slot on the side of the Probe and pushed the button to reprogram the chip. Only took a few minutes to complete.

They swapped out and put the second one in, then she had him reassemble both transmitters.

As they were finishing up, the hatch opened and one of the junior enlisted crew slipped her head in for a moment, nodding and putting a small package on the table, then withdrawing without a word.

Nyssa turned to Garber questioningly.

"Orders from the First Officer," he said, opening the pack and drawing out a pair of Type Three Personal Disruptors, deadly eggs he rested in his big hand. "These are going down with the transmitters."

Nyssa nodded.

Maybe she needed to learn how to shoot better, too?

19

Padraig had risen early, hardly able to sleep last night to the point he figured he might as well get up and review anything that Chance had left him.

Not much, but he didn't know if that was her handling things competently up on the ship, like normal, or a lack of issues that had come up.

So he ended up starting that novel. Then falling into it to the point that his alarm beeping nearly levitated him out of the chair in surprise before he processed that it was time to go meet Zarah and whoever thought they'd be joining him for breakfast.

Padraig found himself wound to a higher pitch than normal as he drew a breath and faced the door. Probably the gunfights and vehicle chases from the book, and not the situation at hand.

He checked his pockets once our of general superstition.

Money, personal transmitter, attitude problem. Everything a sailor on leave needed to get through the day.

He looked both ways in the hall, but it was empty. Early,

with the sun just starting to brighten the eastern sky out behind the curtains he hadn't pulled back.

Padraig moved to Zarah's hatch and rapped lightly. She must have been just as wound up, because she opened it almost immediately.

They shared a silent, knowing grin, then she fell in beside him as they headed towards the stairs.

The hotel had a lift, but sailors were too superstitious about such things to use them until they had to. Too easy to get trapped if the hull kinked in combat and pinched the tunnel.

Easier to run up and down stairs and ladders all the time getting between decks.

They got downstairs quickly and made their way to the restaurant across an empty lobby. A few folks were eating, but seemed to be outnumbered by the staff.

They got seated quickly and Padraig made sure he and Zarah both had their backs towards the corner, letting them see the rest of the room easily.

He had no idea what to expect.

Breakfast options were heavy on vegetables and fruit, with a variety of pastry options. Not much meat protein, but that was fine. He could have something heavier for lunch for a week, while pretending to be a tourist.

If anybody was really fooled around here.

Juice fortified with vitamins and caffeine was a novel option, but sounded better than most coffee variants, so he tried it. Orange-ish. Sort of. Sweet lime and smooth apple flavor, somehow combined.

A man appeared at the door and nodded to the hostess as he walked by, making a beeline toward Padraig's table. Padraig hadn't told the woman he was expecting a third, but she didn't seem to mind.

Or had been warned ahead of time.

Snappy dresser. Baggy slacks with pinstripes matched a double-breasted jacket, both in a muted green just this side of olive. Mint shirt with a bright green tie. He almost looked like a fairy from some tale, dressed up for a modern retelling.

Male. Middle-aged and a little squishy around the middle. Local from his coloration. Receding hairline not to the top yet, but thinking about it strongly.

He came to rest a meter away from the table and smiled.

"Harley Gomez," he introduced himself, then went ahead and pulled out a third chair to sit.

Padraig watched his hand come to rest on the table, lift long enough to reveal a bronze coin broken into two pieces, before the hand covered it again and it vanished.

Padraig nodded.

"I got your note last night," he replied evenly. "How may we be of assistance?"

"Joshua was a friend of mine," Gomez replied with a quiet heat. "Drinking buddy. Raconteur. Gourmand. You name it, he did it, and did it well. I want the bastards who did this to him taken down."

Padraig watched the man's face go from *bonhomie* to ruthless as he finished, then back to friendly just as quickly.

"I'm an outsider here, Gomez," Padraig reminded him, as it felt like everybody else was several chapters ahead of him in the story with what they thought Padraig was going to do. "The Governor asked me to look into things. I'm not some samurai badass come to town to kill people for whatever crimes the locals think they committed. The law can arrest them and handle it."

Gomez studied him closely. Still smiling, but there was a feral edge to it.

"If those folks were any good, they'd have already arrested whoever did it," Gomez nodded. "Hesell's got you out there as a bird dog."

"Likely," Padraig agreed without heat. "Doesn't change anything. I'm beginning to wonder if he is mostly using me to flip over rocks for him, to see what was hiding underneath."

Gomez's face went perfectly still for a moment, then brightened. He laughed.

"Josh would've loved you, Boru," he said.

Then everything fell to silence as the waiter started heading their direction, making enough noise to make sure everyone knew he was coming.

Padraig wondered if Harley Gomez was known to the staff personally. Or if he had that big of a reputation around Ilham.

Nobody Padraig knew, but didn't that describe most of the planet?

They ordered. Padraig went heavy on salad options, pretty much adding everything. Zarah stayed with a local pastry and juice.

"I'll have my usual," Gomez informed the waiter, establishing clearly that he was a known quantity, at least that much.

Nat that he was anybody Padraig knew. Nor was Padraig particularly certain that he wanted to know the man. At least so far.

"Tell me about Joshua Wrezal," Padraig dared the man when they were alone again.

Somewhere, someone dialed up the background music from muted to loud enough to cover some conversation. The staff understanding that Harley Gomez wanted his business quiet?

"You're going to hear all sorts of bad things about the man," Gomez nodded. "Mostly, that's sour grapes, because he was short, balding, and pudgy, and yet every woman on the planet wanted him to take her to bed. And a lot of the men."

"Why was that?" Zarah spoke up sharply. "What made him so compelling?"

"One of the most charming bastards you'll ever meet," Gomez nodded to her. "Eloquent. Funny. Friendly. And he had a rep as a lover that had gotten around, so the ladies approved of him."

"Did his wife kill him?" Zarah asked. "If he was busy with every other woman around?"

"Eliana is a jewel," Gomez shook his head. "An utter doll. Stayed home for the most part, only going out with Josh enough to remind folks that she'd landed him, and everyone else was just borrowing the man for a brief time. They had an arrangement where Joshua kept things generally quiet while he wandered off and enjoyed himself."

"If he was that compelling, why was he clear the hell out here at Monsanch?" Padraig asked. "Wouldn't he have been better back at the *Traisa* capital at Zulou?"

Gomez's face turned serious. He took a drink of his juice and swallowed it slowly, like a man savoring the finest wine.

"You didn't hear this from me," Gomez said quietly, scowling at Padraig as he spoke.

Padraig nodded.

"Bad blood at Zulou," Gomez nodded, referring to *Traisa*'s capital world. "Enough to get him exiled out here."

"With whom?" Padraig pressed. "Sounds to me like that's where we might start looking."

Gomez's grimace was pure pain.

"Josh never talked," he said. "Didn't kiss and tell. Nothing like that. He did get drunk one night and a little maudlin. Grumbled about things back home."

Gomez fell silent there and Padraig watched the man. Weighing odds, it seemed.

The silence stretched.

Gomez finally shrugged.

"I got the impression—and mind you, this is all speculation on my part with distant hindsight—that there were folks pissed back home that Eliana had chosen Josh over maybe a more prominent candidate," Gomez explained.

Padraig paused before replying. If Wrezal was that popular and charming, then Monsanch had probably been something of an exile for the man.

Which suggested who might have exiled him. And why.

"Arodd Torray?" Padraig asked, naming the Supreme Autocrat himself.

The man in charge of the *Enlightened Tyranny of Traisa* itself.

Gomez nodded, then clamped his mouth shut and watched.

Padraig understood the man's sudden reticence. Even this many light-years separation might not be enough to protect someone from those sorts of killers, if the Supreme Autocrat of *Traisa* decided to make it *personal*.

At the same time, Padraig doubted that there was anything he might be able to do at that point, if one assumed some level of diplomatic immunities involved. Gomez seemed to be suggesting that Wrezal's own people might have killed him.

Using the confusion of a new *A'Zedi* embassy's arrival to move?

That was a good way to make an enemy of Padraig Boru, but there wasn't much he could do or say. *Traisa* was an ally.

At least for now, he corrected himself.

The *Holy Imperium of Copez* had been *Wronlori*'s ally in the previous war. It had taken a new Archbishop to change those alliances to make them *A'Zedi*'s friend today.

Padraig sipped his juice and tried to remember any details about Arodd Torray. He knew the man was about a decade and a half older than Padraig, so right around fifty, but not much more than that.

Traisa used something of an elected imperial model for their government, with the strongest candidate generally ascending to power when the previous died in office or retired because they'd been too ground down by the business.

Or killed in a palace coup.

At the end of the *War of the Third Alliance* eight year ago, the former Supreme Autocrat had been deposed. Or retired. Allowed to retire, maybe. In any case, replaced by Arodd Torray when the former man was used up and done.

Food arrived and they ate in a bristly silence, broken only by passing butter and salt around the table.

By the time the food was done, more people had begun to arrive in the restaurant. Outside, the sun should be over the horizon, though most folks didn't go into an office for a few hours yet.

The waiter cleared the empty tables and refilled juice.

Padraig eyed Gomez as they were alone again.

"Who are you, Harley Gomez?" he asked bluntly. "What makes you so angry and intent on revenge here?"

"Josh was my friend," Gomez snarled quietly. "He didn't care about your birth or your wealth. How pretty you were or how ugly. Only that you were an interesting person, and therefore worth spending time with. Monsanch is a quiet, private place. Folks with money like to keep an unwritten caste system in place, to let little folks like me know our place, but Joshua invited a wide range of ideas and interests to his parties, dinner or otherwise. Whoever killed him might not be working for the local powers-that-be, but that person did them a favor, because Joshua Wrezal had done more to break down social barriers on this world than anybody I know."

Padraig considered his words carefully.

"Do you have the money to step in and replace him?" Padraig asked.

"Me?" Gomez jerked backwards in surprise.

"If someone keeps having these dinners and parties, then he won't be entirely lost," Padraig continued. "If certain folks don't wish to participate, maybe you need to make sure that your parties are such that they are the ones missing out, and not you."

He watched a different gleam come into the man's eyes. Shrewd. Calculating.

Padraig would have said criminal, but he didn't know the man well enough to cast aspersions. At the same time, he didn't think he'd be all that wrong.

"Your new ambassador," Gomez replied. "The lush babe with pretty smile and the infectious laugh. She's an outsider. Would she be willing to help?"

Padraig considered it.

"I can ask," he replied. "You might have to charm her yourself, like Josh would have done. At the same time, *A'Zedi* wants to make better friends with Monsanch. And not just the money and power, but all the people. Maybe that needs to be your approach when you ask her."

"I like you, Boru," Gomez said. "You're all right people. You talk to her, and I'll follow up in a few days to see if I can put together the right kind of party. Josh would want us to throw him the sort of wake that eventually involved the police department, the fire department, and maybe every journalist on the planet. Sounds like we should do exactly that."

Padraig watched him reach into his pocket and palm something, then reach out to shake hands.

There was something in his hand that he passed on. Small and jagged.

"In case you need to verify a messenger later," Gomez said as he rose. "I'll be in touch."

Padraig nodded, uncertain what he might have just walked into, but supposing that it would be good, on balance.

"Oh, and breakfast is on me," Gomez smiled as he nodded to both of them. "Captain. Squire. Pleasure to make your acquaintance."

Then he turned and walked away.

Padraig glanced at half of a bronze coin, then closed his fist around it.

"What just happened?" Zarah asked.

"Damned if I know," Padraig replied.

20

Chance happened to be standing a shift on the bridge, mostly because having Padraig and Zarah down on the surface meant the ship would be stretched pretty thin for officers if she didn't. And to stay in touch with people. Frequently, her battle station was aft, so she didn't have as good a relationship with everyone forward as Padraig did.

That was changing. And she had started rotating officers and enlisted forward and aft this week while getting ready.

Bex Magorian was forward this shift. She was focused on her boards watching Radio, her strawberry blonde hair almost throwback to the *Enlightened Tyranny of Traisa*.

She looked up sharply and her eyes got serious.

Chance watched her silently.

Bex typed several commands into her board, read the results, then typed some more.

Finally she looked up at Chance.

"Nyssa Taggart is kinda scary," Bex announced simply.

"Why?"

"*Traisa* just got a message on the ground," Bex replied.

"Transmission from Zulou itself. I wonder if I read it faster than the folks below us did."

"What's it say?" Chance asked.

"They acknowledge the assassination of Ambassador Wrezal," Bex said. "Order his deputy to execute the office briefly, because the man's replacement is already *en route*."

"*En route*?" Chance clarified.

"Affirmative, Commander," Bex nodded. "Already selected, assigned, and in transit on the heels of the message."

Chance leaned back and considered various responses.

"How close is the package to being delivered to Captain Boru?" she pressed.

Bex stopped and typed several commands.

"Shuttle is on the ground now," she muttered. "ETA any moment, from the looks of things."

"Ping it for a response," Chance ordered. "He needs to know immediately. If I'm out of contact, pass along the contents of that message to him when he calls. When you go off duty, whoever replaces you to do the same until we confirm that Captain Boru knows."

"Understood, sir," Bex said.

Chance watched her start typing.

Wrezal hadn't been dead a week, and they already had a replacement flying out here from Zulou?

Usually, something like that took a month to sort out, even after you had identified a candidate, as they would need to have their security clearance updated. Then brief said person about the new mission. Get them packed up for a long stint away from the capital. *Et cetera*.

A lot of work that only showed up in the vast amount of paperwork involved. The quiet things bureaucracies did to make the galaxy turn.

Chance checked the local time. Late morning below them, after Padraig had spoken with the bishop last night, then had some breakfast meeting today that he wasn't going to discuss until he had the new personal transmitter in his hand.

Operating in the dark.

She went ahead and dialed a number on her armrest console.

"Wardroom."

"First Officer on the bridge," Chance replied. "Please go ahead and send up a fresh carafe of coffee. Feels like a long day ahead."

"Understood, Commander."

She cut the line.

If the folks back in *Traisa* were that far ahead of the bureaucratic curve, they probably hadn't been surprised by the assassination.

Had they been the ones who ordered it?

21

Padraig considered his options.

"Should I be going with you?" Zarah asked.

"Negative," Padraig decided. "I'd like you to spend some time at the library, digging into recent or modern history of Monsanch."

He paused for a moment, seeking the words, then saw them on the table next to his chair, where he and Zarah had retired after breakfast.

"Or modern fiction," he added.

Zarah turned to look at him confused.

"Sir?" she asked. "What am I looking for?"

"I'm not sure I can describe it adequately," Padraig grimaced. "Who is Monsanch? What are they like as a people and a culture? Who are they at home, and who do they tell themselves they want to be?"

Zarah's eyes got a distant look.

"Okay," she nodded. "You might be better off having Nyssa along next time for something like that, though."

"Possibly, but don't sell yourself short, Zarah," he replied. "I wouldn't have brought you down if I didn't think you could handle it. And this is the sort of research task an officer three days out of Uni should be perfectly prepared to undertake."

She blushed and grinned. That was frequently how she described herself, as she'd only joined the ship's crew a month before their first mission to Albany, and those orders had been cut literally three days after she'd been commissioned.

"Now?" she asked.

"Now," he agreed.

Except that someone rapped on his door. Padraig turned deadly serious as he rose, gesturing Zarah out of sight in the washroom. If someone rushed him, they'd end up with her behind them.

Not that he was expecting violence, but Ilham had already shown itself to be a far more complicated place than he'd expected.

And it only promised to get weirder.

He peeked through a fisheye lens at the hallway, recognizing Specialist Glen Tameron standing there in civilian clothing, rather than the mulberry and mauve of an *A'Zedi* uniform.

Padraig pulled the bolt and opened the door.

Tameron stepped forward, unslinging a messenger bag to pull out a small bundle that he passed to Padraig without a word, turning and walking away without once looking back.

Padraig poked his head out to look both ways, but didn't see anyone.

He stepped back and closed the hatch, then set the bolt again.

Moving to the table, he unwrapped the bundle as Zarah emerged and joined him.

She gasped, but he'd specifically asked Chance to send

down some Type Threes as well when he delivered new transmitters. Padraig handed her one.

"You will have this with you at all times, Squire," he ordered. "Including in the shower as well. Am I clear?"

"Yes, sir," she nodded, a little more pale than she had been.

"Good," Padraig nodded and handed her a new transmitter. "Off you go and stay in touch."

"Will do, Captain," she said, moving to the door and exiting.

Padraig returned to his chair to sit and think. And give her a head start.

His unit beeped once, then a red light began strobing on and off every second.

"Boru," he said, keying it live.

"Messier," Chance replied. "I have an update."

"Go ahead," Padraig said.

"We expect that a replacement ambassador from Zulou in *Traisa* is already in flight, Captain," Chance said. "ETA unknown, but we expect to be able to refine that as better intelligence becomes available."

Padraig cursed under his breath.

"There's more," Chance continued. "Didn't want to say this last night over what might have been an unsecured line, but there was a message sent by the *Traisa* embassy some ninety minutes after Wrezal was killed. The message was simply *'It's done.'* and was encoded at the time."

Which suggested strongly that Nyssa Taggart really had managed to break one of the *Enlightened Tyranny*'s main diplomatic encryption systems. How dangerous was that, at least until those folks realized it and changed things? Could he read messages sent home by that embassy?

Or at least Chance could. And she was probably even

better at parsing bureaucratic warfare than he was, having spent several years behind a desk until her kids were old enough for her to return to warship duty.

"Keep me posted on things," Padraig ordered. "I'm planning to show up at the front gate of the *Wronlori* embassy in a bit and ask for a meeting."

"Is that wise?" Chance countered.

He understood her conservatism on the topic. *A'Zedi* was at war with *Wronlori*. Again. Maybe still, as the *United Technocracy* only seemed to withdraw each time long enough to rebuild their fleets before attacking again. At least over the last generation.

"Monsanch is an *Unaffiliated* world," Padraig reminded her. "Neutral ground, as it were. This might be a once in a lifetime chance for me to actually talk to someone from their worlds in a friendly enough setting. Plus, everyone already seems to know what I'm about, so I doubt I'll accomplish much as an investigator."

"Palace leaks?" Chance asked.

"Assuredly," Padraig replied. "I want to go on the offensive here and see if I can use that to my advantage."

"Be careful," Chance admonished him, sounding more like a mom than a First Officer.

But she was both. And this was an inherently dangerous profession.

"Will do," he acknowledged. "Zarah is hitting the library. I'll check in again when I'm done with *Wronlori*."

"Understood."

Padraig cut the line and stood up. Instead of reading, maybe he'd walk some, paying better attention in case someone tried to slip a note into his pocket.

How many people were watching his every step?
And how could he get them to trip over each other?

22

Padraig had been indoors, and not paying that much attention, so the sudden, sharp chill as he emerged from the hotel caught him by surprise. At least ten degrees cooler than yesterday. Almost enough to cut through his jacket.

Folks around him were better bundled up, but he supposed that most of them were used to weather. Or had read the forecast.

Starships were climate controlled to a specific setting at all times. And he generally kept *Marrakesh* warmer than other ships he'd served on, because the female half of his crew appreciated not freezing or having to wear extra layers while on duty.

And it was downright cold outside this morning.

Rather than dawdle, he stretched his legs and stayed close to the buildings as he walked, trying to escape the breeze that kissed his hands and nose with ice.

The *Wronlori* Embassy, like the *Holy Imperium*'s cathedral, took up most of a block. Waist-high brick wall below, with three meters of wrought iron fence above that, revealing a well-manicured lawn and trees surrounding buildings inside the fence, though most folks were indoors.

Several Ilham police officers stood around outside the main gate, but didn't challenge him as he went up and into a hollow courtyard, where four *Wronlori* naval troopers stood at attention.

Padraig addressed himself to the oldest one with a smile as he came to rest. All four watched him indifferently.

"My name is Padraig Boru," he told the man. "I'm a captain with the *A'Zedi* navy and I'd like to arrange a meeting with Ambassador Jenker if she's available."

He had their attention now. The trooper in charge blinked several times as his brain caught up with Padraig's words.

"Stand by," he managed, suddenly sharp and pointing to a nearby corner. "You wait there."

Padraig nodded and shifted over, keeping his hands in plain sight and a smile on his face as he came to rest. Two of the troopers watched him while the third watched the street.

The one in charge stepped back, opened a hatch in the wall, and slipped inside.

It was freaking cold out today. At least he was in a protected space, so the wind wasn't biting.

Still, he would need to get something hot to drink soon, either here or at a nearby coffee shop.

He waited.

Padraig supposed that no news was good, so he exercised patience. It should have been a surprise, and he had no doubt that his arrival was being bounced quickly to the top of the chain of command.

Hopefully, he'd caught everyone off guard.

That thought kept the smile on his face.

Eventually, the hatch opened and the trooper returned,

with a new bureaucrat in tow. The man moved to a bodyguard position, while the young woman addressed herself to Padraig.

Slim. Mid-twenties, if he had to guess, but they'd been easy years. Not attractive. Not homely. Not his type either way.

"Captain Boru?" she asked.

He nodded and smiled even broader.

"This is highly irregular," she observed.

"Indeed," he agreed. "And probably entirely necessary. Is she available?"

The woman blinked several times.

"You'll go through a full security screening before you are allowed inside."

"Understood." He turned to the senior trooper. "I have a small disruptor in my left jacket pocket at the waist. And a personal transmitter on the right side. Should I pull them out or would you prefer to?"

The trooper turned to the woman and got her nod.

"I'll handle it, sir," he said.

Padraig held himself still as the man circled behind him. A hand found the transmitter first, then the Type Three. They would be hard pressed to access the transmitter, at least without leaving obvious traces. And he could always ask Taggart to send down another one.

Might be necessary after this, but he'd been playing things by ear anyway.

"Anything else?" the man asked in Padraig's ear.

"Identification papers and some cash," Padraig replied. "Should show up on your scanner, but I wanted you on top of things here."

"Very good, sir," he said.

Hands quickly patted down pockets, belt, and ankles.

"He's clear."

The woman nodded, still somewhat off-kilter by the turn of events.

"This way, Captain Boru," she said, turning and opening the hatch.

He followed her into a small building, where a dozen armed troops watched him with nervous care.

More than he would have expected for an embassy like this. Or were they less popular with the locals than he'd anticipated, and had to maintain a small strike force at all times? He didn't think his arrival was *that* dangerous.

Still, that thought added to his smile. It gave Sana Alkes another opening to exploit later.

Another senior trooper gestured Padraig to a spot on the floor with boot prints painted.

"Stand on the spot with your hands over your head and remain still," the man ordered.

Padraig complied, smiling. Cheerful, even.

Everything that disturbed *Wronlori*, however little, he would count as a win. But he had a petty side and wasn't about to deny it.

Most of the troops watched him. Several had hands on weapons. He couldn't fault their professional paranoia.

He'd have acted almost exactly the same, were the situation reversed.

Maybe he'd get that lucky, one of these days.

The scan went fine. Nobody reacted. Padraig waited.

"This way, Captain Boru," the woman finally said, after one of the technicians behind a counter nodded.

Padraig fell in, unsurprised when four of the naval troopers split off and surrounded him as he went.

If nothing else, he was giving their security system a workout this morning. All by himself.

They exited the building, crossed a short arcade through blustery winds, and went into the main portion of the embassy.

Someone had spent a lot of money in here. No, he corrected himself. Someone had understood how to spend a lot of money and do it quite well.

Blue-gray marble floors and walls. Dark wood beams upheld a vaulted roof six meters high, creating a vast, airy feel inside. Plants in pots and furniture arranged in small conversational clusters gave the volume a warm, homey feel. Fireplace burning real wood along one wall.

"This way," she said, drawing him past the space and up a broad staircase with a carpet down the center and oil paintings on the walls.

All four goons kept pace, moving almost as quietly as Padraig did.

His smile was unrelenting. Almost a weapon in and of itself.

It would be rude to tell them how much he was enjoying all this. However accurate.

The woman led him to a closed door, knocked twice, then opened it enough to stick her head inside.

Some quiet conversation occurred, then she pushed the door the rest of the way in and gestured him to follow.

And all four of his friends.

The space turned out to be an oversized office. Almost a major conference room, but it was definitely a personal working space, with a desk at one end, couches in the middle, and a lot of open volume.

Ambassador Brina Jenker rose from behind the desk.

He'd seen pictures of the woman, but they hadn't done her justice, even as much as they had.

Tall. Not quite his height, but not far shorter. Lean and elegant build, shown off by the work of an excellent tailor.

Silky, curly, ash-gray hair was worn shoulder length and reminded him of nothing so much as a waterfall.

Her skin was darker than normal for *Wronlori*, closer in brown to his than the paler or golden tones of the *United Technocracy*.

She had a broad, almost domed forehead and wide eyes that looked like sapphires. Laugh lines suggested a mature woman in her late forties. Not fashion model beautiful, but possessed of a warm charisma that filled the room in a manner similar to the scent of roses he suspected was her perfume.

"Captain Boru," she said as she rose. "This is an unexpected surprise."

She moved like a savvy alley cat as she came around the desk and took his hand where he'd come to rest in the middle of her space.

"I felt like it was an opportunity too good to miss," he replied, still smiling, but not as open and bright.

"You look cold, Captain," she observed. "Can I get you something? Tea? Hot chocolate?"

"Warm, yes," he said. "Hot chocolate would be marvelous."

She gestured to the woman that Padraig took to be her aide, then settled the two of them on facing couches.

All four guards took up positions like hawks around him, which just caused the smile to return.

This wasn't starship combat. He was no threat to the ambassador whatsoever.

But keeping everyone off-balance did wonders to improve his humor.

"What brings you to my door, Captain Boru?" she asked as

she kicked off her shoes and curled her legs underneath herself like a cat.

Padraig looked around to make eye contact with his guards. And smile. They were all set to tackle him at the slightest provocation.

"I've had a chance to speak with several players about Joshua Wrezal," he began. "Since we're all on neutral ground here, I thought I should avail myself of the opportunity to consult you, Ambassador. Did you know Ambassador Wrezal all that well?"

Her smile was warm and knowing. Perhaps revealing more than words would. But hadn't Gomez said that he could charm any woman into his bed? Or himself into hers?

How close had he and Ambassador Jenker been? And was that another reason to have him killed?

"Joshua threw the most interesting parties, Captain," she replied with a laugh. Not evasive, but not revealing anything. "I'm just sorry you'll never get a chance to attend one, as they were quite intellectually stimulating. He and I knew each other professionally, of course, but the wars of the rims were far less worrisome here."

Padraig nodded. About as he'd expected. Everyone was a great distance from their capitals, including him. And seemed to be operating on a different wavelength.

How much of that had been Wrezal's doing, if everyone seemed to like the man?

Everyone except whoever shot him to death, of course. There was always that.

"I've heard a great deal about the man's many friends," Padraig continued. "Who were his enemies?"

He didn't figure he could possibly get a straight answer, but her evasions or deflections would be almost as revealing.

Ambassador Jenker's face turned a bit more serious. Not hostile. Scholarly, perhaps.

"I'm not certain Joshua had enemies," she began, then waved a hand as he opened his mouth. "The Ambassador from *Traisa* certainly did, but I think we ought to talk about them as two separate people, if that makes sense."

Padraig nodded.

"I had a meeting that suggested he could charm any woman and most men," Padraig replied. "Was he a threat to the local power structure because he was so capable of putting people at ease? So friendly. Making them forget that they were supposed to be enemies, at a time when folks would prefer that?"

Technically, this woman was his enemy. At the same time, *Unaffiliated* meant neutral.

Her brow furrowed in the cutest way.

"Who have you been talking to?" she asked, confused and curious.

"Someone who already misses the man," Padraig replied discreetly. "Who perhaps appreciated what he did to bring people together in a single room and get them to talk. Rather like I'm doing, but I do not have his charm. I'm merely a man looking into a murder."

Her eyes got a faraway look.

"I can see why Hesell asked you to get involved," she said with a nod, confirming that if the Governor hadn't simply broadcast that conversation on local airwaves, someone on his staff functionally had.

Did everyone here know what Padraig was up to? If so, what the hell did they think he'd accomplish?

Except that he'd already drawn in several players, all of them interested. Concerned. Committed, perhaps.

The young woman returned with a mug of hot chocolate that she put on the coffee table, then withdrew to a corner.

Padraig wasn't worried about secrets. He didn't know enough to have any, save that Nyssa was at least as smart as he'd suspected. And more than she'd herself realized.

Padraig sipped. Real chocolate. Real everything, rather than a mix you added hot water to and stirred, like he had on the ship.

Diplomats lived richer lives than starship captains. He'd seen that on the flight out, when Sana Alkes had two restaurants serving her aboard the Starliner module.

He perked up. Ambassador Jenker did as well. Her goons flinched, but that couldn't be helped.

"What was Joshua's favorite restaurant?" he asked innocently.

Had he tossed a live hedgehog onto the table to waddle around, Padraig wasn't sure he could top the amount of confusion he could see on the faces around him.

His smile was so unrelenting that he figured his face muscles would hurt later.

A man was dead, and this should be a serious task, but Padraig didn't have to be a morose son of a bitch in the process. From all he'd heard so far, Joshua Wrezal would have appreciated that someone was smiling.

Ambassador Jenker stared at him in confusion.

"Where did the man go to celebrate life?" Padraig continued. "Or to have one of these amazing dinner parties I've heard so much about?"

Might as well let her know that he'd talked to a lot of people. If nothing else, that would confuse the watchers even more.

And more and more, that seemed to be why Hesell had

brought him in.

What else were you supposed to do when someone hands you a blank piece of paper and shrugs?

"Antonov's," she replied after a moment, still uncertain where he was headed. "Why?"

Padraig was uncertain, but as had been pointed out, he might be merely the stalking horse here. Who could he flush out into the open?

"You are not the first person to point out how much I missed, never getting a chance to know the man," Padraig replied. "I'd like to get some sort of feel for him, especially as I'm looking into the circumstances of his death."

"Do you think you'll be able to solve it, when the complete law enforcement apparatus of Ilham has failed?" she replied in a haughtier tone.

But then, she might have finally remembered that she represented *Wronlori*, and he was an *A'Zedi* naval officer. Her technical enemy.

Hopefully, nobody had gotten around to telling these folks about *Sundering Wrath* and his adventures at Albany.

Padraig fixed her with a calm eye. And that smile that really seemed to bewilder everyone else.

"I have a mission," he told the woman bluntly. "I intend to pursue that mission until it is complete, or I'm ordered otherwise. As to the rest, if I can continue to bother you for a bit, I'd hoped to get your impressions of the man, rather than the ambassador. I can assume all the technical sides of things, but the personal intrigues me."

She blinked and he watched her brain reset. Her emotions. Her intentions.

"Joshua was a scamp in the best ways..." she began, as Padraig leaned back and sipped his hot chocolate.

23

Padraig's smile was unrelenting. After an hour of talking to Brina Jenker, she'd loaned him a wrap somewhere between a cape and a cloak for length. Being *Wronlori*, he'd almost expected it to be the same taupe as their uniforms, darker than sand but lighter than brown.

Instead, this one was a darker blue, covering him head to calf and keeping the wind from biting as hard. More importantly, it kept him dry, as a steady drizzle had crept in while he'd been talking to her.

He had the hood up as he opened the door and entered the darker space, careful to lower the hood without throwing water every which way.

A middle-aged man stood behind a lectern and watched as Padraig slipped out of the cloak and looked for a place to hang it.

"We'll handle that, sir," the man said, holding out a hand. "Lunch for one?"

"I have a reservation," Padraig replied, handing it to him. "Boru."

"Ah, Captain Boru, welcome," the man said.

The manager snapped his fingers and handed the dripping cloth to a young woman who had almost materialized next to him, then grabbed a menu.

"This way, Captain."

Padraig followed.

Brina Jenker had made the reservation in his name. And apparently played the same game as Hesell, making Padraig seem bigger than he really was.

There was simply no way to live up to the reputation that was growing up around him.

Padraig stumbled to a halt and nearly staggered.

"Sir?" the manager asked, eyes concerned now as he stopped and took a step closer.

"I'm fine," Padraig lied, drawing a breath deep and focusing on projecting an image that he wanted the others to absorb.

It got him seated, with a promise of coffee. More importantly, it provided him a few moments of privacy to rethink that last image.

Living up to a reputation.

He'd just spent an hour talking to Brina Jenker, hearing about the Joshua Wrezal who threw amazing parties and seemingly befriended everyone and anyone. Then there was Ambassador Wrezal, representing the Supreme Autocrat's interests, however many light-centuries distant from the closest *Traisa* system.

Who was Joshua Wrezal, the man?

Did *anyone* know?

Padraig found himself wondering if anyone really did. Perhaps Eliana, the newly minted widow? She put up with the performances and affairs. Was she privy to the inner man, in ways nobody else was?

Padraig doubted that he'd be allowed to interview her. Not without an exceptionally compelling reason that he currently lacked.

What reason would compel? Padraig wondered how quickly she would be bundled up and sent home, now that her husband was dead and a replacement already in transit to Monsanch.

That thought suddenly chilled him to the bone.

Joshua Wrezal had been assassinated. Everyone had been focusing on that fact.

Even Padraig had been wrapped up in the why, expecting that the man had enemies on Monsanch.

What if none of this had anything to do with Ambassador Wrezal, save that he was married to Eliana? Gomez had hinted at secrets even he hadn't known. Taggart had read a message that could ambiguously point at *Traisa* themselves doing the deed.

Why?

His waitress intruded before Padraig's thought processes bore fruit.

He studied her. Thirty-something, so roughly Padraig's age, he thought. Smart look in her eyes as she studied him back.

"I'm here to celebrate the life of my friend Joshua Wrezal," Padraig told her.

"Oh, the ambassador!" she replied with a smile, before her face saddened.

Padraig nodded solemnly.

"What would Joshua have ordered, were he here with me today?" Padraig asked.

Her eyes got a distant look to them.

"Let me talk to the cook," she said. "He'll understand. It isn't on the menu."

Then she turned and walked away without another word. Padraig nodded.

Not on the menu. Sounded an awful lot like a man known for coloring outside the lines. And charming folks, even strangers.

How much of that might rub off on Padraig, as he delved deeper into this civilization?

She returned a few moments later with coffee, as well as a thimble glass of red wine.

"He always started with port," she intoned with great seriousness, as though on a holy mission. "And the chef agreed, so I'll start bringing plates out shortly."

Padraig had no idea what he was in for. Save that Joshua would have ordered it, had he been here today.

Padraig took the glass and silently toasted the man he'd never met, as though he was seated directly across the table.

Unlike the wine Governor Hesell had been serving, it was smooth and sweet and pleasant to imbibe.

He found himself looking forward to whatever his lunch was about to be.

24

Padraig had arrived at the early side of lunch, when Antonov's was still somewhat empty. By the time he had waded through a selection of small dishes prepared with love and care, the room was nearly full.

Thus, he didn't realize who the man approaching was until Governor Hesell pulled out the chair across from him and sat with a secretive grin on his face.

The waitress was there a moment later, eyes huge as she recognized the governor.

"Coffee, and one of whatever that dessert is," Hesell told her, pointing at Padraig's—hopefully—last plate, a berried custard that had been flashed with a blowtorch in front of him to crystallize the surface without warming it.

Padraig smiled. He'd eaten too much, even when most of the plates were smaller than the saucer his coffee sat in. Many of the empty plates still surrounded him like asteroids.

And he had a much better appreciation of who Joshua Wrezal was.

Hesell smiled back. The noise around them wasn't enough to smother conversations, but someone would have to be at a handful of nearby tables to hear anything.

"I'm given to understand that you've been rather busy since you landed," Hesell said obliquely, eyes laughing.

Padraig chuckled at the understatement. The farmers market. The woman selling books. Skye Bancroft and her Bishop. Harley Gomez. Brina Jenker.

Plus, a seemingly never-ending selection of small plate delicacies better than even Sana Alkes had been served shipboard by her own staff.

And it was only now approaching local noon. He still had a bit before he'd been on the surface for a full day.

Padraig put his spoon down halfway through the custard and sipped some coffee to focus his mind. A nap sounded really good right about now, but that was the oncoming food coma. He'd never had a meal anywhere near as amazing to this, and it had been the sort of off-menu thing that Joshua would order?

Truly, an exceptional man.

"I have learned many interesting things," Padraig replied. Not evasive, merely unable to encompass Joshua.

At the same time, he expected that Governor Hesell probably knew the key points already.

"Have you now?" Hesell asked, his smile close to matching Padraig's.

"This is not, however, likely the best place to discuss some of them," Padraig nodded to encompass the room around them.

"My office?" Hesell asked.

Padraig didn't balk, but something in his eyes showed.

"You tell me," Hesell nodded after a moment.

Padraig agreed. And the lovely waitress returned with a plate for the governor, so they slipped into silence broken by the sound of spoons scraping up every last bit of custard.

25

Zarah had spent the morning in the library. She had a stack of books on the table in front of her, and the occasional bored or lonely librarians swinging by to check in on her. She had the place to herself with a single, burning question.

Who did Monsanch want to tell itself it really was, when nobody else was around?

That had been Captain Boru's question. She'd spent several hours deep-diving into that very topic, but didn't have solid answers.

What she had were more questions.

The colony was four centuries old at this point, starting with a large lander that had settled on what was now the starport well outside of town. Ilham had been the founding city, set at a safe enough distance from ships losing control on landing, with a river and a fertile, grassy plain nearby.

Folks raised herd animals for meat, hides, and fur. Others farmed. The economy was old enough, stable enough—rich enough—that a few of the wealthier folks were growing nothing but grapes for wine-making, though little of that was exported.

Trade flourished, mostly because Monsanch was the oldest colony in this direction, with several dozen newer ones that had been established closer to the core in the meantime. Folks came to Monsanch from both directions, the larger ships from the rims delivering containers to orbiting warehouses, where things were broken down into smaller shipments to be delivered by a variety of smaller companies and tramp freighters.

Taxation was light, largely because the scales were enormous enough that even a tiny percentage added up quickly.

Zarah found herself surprised that nobody had ever tried to conquer Monsanch and add it to their own nation as a new frontier, headed inwards towards the core. At the same time, nobody was close, though *A'Zedi* was the closest nation. Concurrently, it was a thin margin to *Copez*'s nearest system.

There was still a serious haul involved to get here.

Not much in the way of actual piracy, but she put that down to all of the stations being armed enough to destroy anything that moved and threatened them.

She looked over at some of the fiction she'd grabbed, not quite at random, but following a scent she couldn't have explained to someone.

Who were their heroes? That was another facet of the Captain's question.

Monsanch had a lot of stories about young Turks putting it over on the megacorporations from the rim nations. Folks from *A'Zedi* and *Wronlori* for the most part, who were inevitably faceless villains until they threatened the locals, almost like the ancient melodramas.

Distrust of outsiders seemed to be a solid thread that ran through many of them.

When she'd found a list of local bestseller books, Zarah had also noted how frequently the heroes were tramp freighter captains who tended to make their money by smuggling on the side.

Always, though, at the cost of the *A'Zedi* and *Wronlori* industrial conglomerates who were screwing the little people on Monsanch or the coreward worlds.

That solid distrust of outsiders. Almost verging on loathing.

Given three hours of looking, she still couldn't determine if Monsanch was going to become the core of a new star nation, in a manner like how *A'Zedi* and *Traisa* had both split off from the place that would later become *Wronlori*.

At the same time, she was willing to hazard a guess that the other colonies around here were likely just as stiff-necked and proud of their individualism. Just as difficult to corral, if you wanted to conquer them and join them to something else.

She didn't know what it meant, but she'd gotten a library card and checked out a few electronic books for herself to read tonight. Tomorrow, she might see about getting herself permanent copies of a few, like the Captain had done. And maybe sending her full report on to him, to transmit to Ambassador Alkes.

Right now, she needed some lunch.

26

Padraig had suggested a walk. Governor Hesell hadn't batted an eye when he agreed. The rain outside had gotten lighter, and the breeze had fallen to almost nothing, but folks were still making a point to stay indoors. That, or walk quickly with their heads down between buildings.

Umbrellas seemed to be a foreign innovation that the locals scoffed at.

Hesell had two bodyguards trailing him at a polite distance that might make someone mistake them for fellow travelers on the same road.

Padraig and Hesell walked north. There was a park and a shopping complex this direction if they went far enough.

"So why didn't you want to talk in my office?" Hesell asked as they crossed the intersection.

"By the time I'd landed, it seemed like every power player in the city knew who I was and what I was up to," Padraig replied quietly. "You are my fourth meeting so far."

"Fourth?" Hesell seemed surprised.

Padraig nodded without enlightening him. If he'd missed someone, hopefully others had as well.

"*Traisa* is the only one I haven't spoken with," Padraig agreed. Then corrected himself. "As yet."

"You assume a leak," Hesell noted. It wasn't a question.

"I guarantee that there is a leak," Padraig smiled. "What I haven't been able to determine is if it was you or someone on your immediate staff, depending on how widely you circulated whatever memo told people what I was up to."

"Me?" Hesell seemed surprised.

"Someone has suggested that I was a stalking horse," Padraig nodded. "I have not seen evidence to refute that. And I don't mind, as everyone has largely been genial so far. I presume that merely means that I'm not getting anywhere close to solving whoever did it."

They walked in silence that stretched long enough to draw Padraig's eyes to the man next to him.

Hesell grinned.

"Sana Alkes said you were smart," the governor nodded. "What do you know?"

Padraig considered the weight of the Type Three disruptor in his pocket. Plus the newly encrypted transmitter on the other side. And the metaphorical weight of this mission on his shoulders.

He'd learned a great deal about Ambassador Wrezal. And the Raconteur. And maybe the man himself, given the luxurious meal that they'd delivered.

Wrezal was a man who dabbled intentionally. Had been. He was dead now, and nobody was willing to admit to being an enemy.

Everyone had enemies. Sometimes they rose to the level of violence, as in this case. Usually, they did not.

"Did you leak my mission?" Padraig asked the man point blank.

"Would it matter?" Hesell countered.

"It might," Padraig told him. "I've come into possession of certain tidbits of knowledge, but I'd rather not end up sharing them with everyone in the city. If it is someone on your staff, even if you told them to do it, I would hope that you might keep a few secrets as I uncover them. Otherwise, I'm probably wasting my time, and that of everyone around me."

Hesell studied him as they walked.

"What have you learned?" the man asked.

"Maybe a why," Padraig answered. "Not a who as yet, but the why might answer that satisfactorily anyway."

They walked in silence.

It stretched to the point that Padraig wondered if he should simply give up and return to his ship. It was one thing to be a stalking horse.

It was something else to walk around with a bullseye on your back.

"I told my staff to leak part of your mission, Boru," Hesell admitted quietly. "As you have surmised, I wanted to see how everyone would react."

"He had more friends than I had anticipated," Padraig acknowledged. "Many of them have reached out because they wanted to see justice done."

Maybe Padraig was stretching the truth a bit. But only a bit. Everyone had excellent things to say about Joshua so far, including an unknown cook in the kitchen at Antonov's that Padraig had never met.

Still, he looked back at the two goons walking nearby. Locked eyes with one.

"Give us a second," he told the man, getting a nod back.

Hesell was studying Padraig closer when he looked back at the governor.

"*Traisa* might have done it themselves," Padraig murmured.

Hesell was shocked. It flashed through his eyes for a moment before settling again.

"What about *Wronlori*?" he asked in quiet voice.

"They might yet be framed for the deed," Padraig acknowledged. "But I just spent an hour with Brina Jenker, hearing her stories about Joshua. Unless she's a completely heartless sociopath of the first order, she liked the man. Even if they were technically enemies."

"Just as the two of you are," Hesell reminded him.

"Just as the two of us are," Padraig agreed. "Who stands to win and lose if the *Enlightened Tyranny*'s ambassador to Monsanch is assassinated?"

"I'm still surprised that you aren't set to blame your traditional enemy, *Wronlori*," Hesell countered.

Padraig shrugged.

"You asked me to look into the assassination," Padraig reminded him. "And semi-unofficially, when you have an entire police authority no doubt investigating, though if I had to guess, the fact that many of your presumed suspects have some level of diplomatic immunity drastically complicates their efforts."

"You have no idea how much that blocks them," Hesell agreed. "I won't say such an investigation is impossible, but at the same time it might come close. For those very reasons."

"Why would you think I could do better?" Padraig asked. "I'm not a diplomat. Merely the captain who delivered Sana Alkes to Monsanch for her mission."

"Because you don't have an ax to grind, Boru," Hesell said.

"When I asked you about some of your adventures at that first event, you didn't come off as a braggart or blowhard, like many other officers tend to. And nobody here knows you yet, so you aren't already tainted by association."

"And thus I could stir things up without bringing my own muddiness?" Padraig asked.

"Close enough," Hesell agreed. "I plan to drop in on things as you move forward, just to see how you are doing."

"Hopefully, I'll have something useful to tell you next time," Padraig said.

"Excellent. Until then."

And with that, Hesell turned right and walked away, both of his bodyguards immediately following and leaving Padraig at a crosswalk. The light changed and he kept heading north.

How soon until this latest secret bit made the rounds?

And who might come after him when it did?

27

Nyssa studied the clock, calculating the offset. Mid-afternoon in the capital city of Ilham. *Marrakesh* was riding low enough in orbit to insert and retrieve *Roadrunner* or *Flight of Fancy* as Commander Messier needed to put a ship on the surface quickly, rather than in a high, geo-synchronous orbit, like normal.

Low enough that she could pick up local transmissions on the ground as they occasionally leaked through the radiation bands that protected the surface of an inhabitable world from the rest of the universe.

Mostly video or audio transmissions. Commercial stuff with advertisements for whoever wanted to reach folks to buy their products. Occasionally, things encrypted via software instead of hardware.

Military equipment used both, scrambling signals via standard code at the same time that they hopped between a pre-calculated set of bands that made it difficult if not impossible to follow unless you had a matching unit to deconstruct.

Hiding a transmission was difficult, if not impossible.

Keeping someone else from reading it was much easier. Especially if you were relying on a simple software scramble and an open channel.

Here, they'd at least done something interesting by bundling the whole thing up as a packet that they squirted. She'd have missed it, but for *Marrakesh* flying low enough that the burst happened to catch her scanners at the right moment, when the clouds parted and let sunlight down.

And radio up.

Nyssa grinned as she typed. In the last week, she'd gotten a serious crash course in advanced cryptographic techniques that was a whole other level above what she'd been doing as the ship's Radio Officer. And it felt like there were several more layers above that, where she was only catching shadows they cast as the ship moved across the sky.

She looked up and noted that Maddox Nevin, an Armiger to her lowly Squire, had command of the ship right now. She was pulling something of a double. Or maybe a triple, depending, but she was young and had the extra energy. Even if Captain Boru was barely fifteen years older than her.

Nevin looked over at her.

"I might need to focus on something to the exclusion of everything else for a bit, sir," she told him. "New signal just came in and it feels important."

He nodded and dialed a number on the armrest of the captain's chair.

"Secondary Bridge. Magorian."

"Bex, Nyssa Taggart is going off-duty immediately to work on a project," Maddox said simply. "You have Radio for the rest of your shift. I'll let you know when she's available again, but you handle everything aft until otherwise ordered."

"Understood, sir," Bex replied. "Assuming Radio duties **now**."

Maddox cut the line and nodded to Nyssa with a helpful smile.

Kind of the big brother she'd never had, growing up, and Nyssa found that all sorts of awesome. She'd spent nineteen years figuring out how to keep everyone else out of her business, when she realized that she was smarter than most of the people she knew.

Now, she had a whole family around her. And this one liked her.

She drew a breath and studied the shape of the file that she'd captured. Why it felt important, she didn't know, other than she'd just spent several days amping up her paranoia to levels that felt like something out of a book.

She'd have liked to have said that the real world never got that weird, but she also knew she'd be lying. Frequently, it was worse, like her commissioned at nineteen and serving as Radio Officer on a warship, less than two years after finishing secondary school.

Escaping, maybe.

Yes, that was it.

Nyssa put her head down and started teasing at the file with some of the new tools she'd written. Stuff out of the cryptographic datacores she'd never imagined existed a month ago.

28

Padraig had checked, and Zarah was just in the process of finishing up a late lunch, so he'd had her return to the hotel, where they could meet up and compare notes. His Personal Transmitter had a short-range sensor built in that looked for other such devices in the immediate vicinity.

Originally, it was to keep two devices from stepping on each other, but Nyssa Taggart had included a note about how he could use it to scan for nearby listening devices if they were giving off a signal.

Padraig didn't like to think about how they had already been reduced to something out of a trashy spy novel, but he wasn't going to argue with his team taking those sorts of precautions.

Monsanch felt like the kind of place where it had become necessary. Right up there with a pistol at hand.

Diplomat at Arms. Hell of a job title. Hell of a responsibility.

A rap at the door to his hotel room and Padraig opened it to let Zarah in. Hopefully, anyone watching who didn't know who she was would mistake her for a girlfriend coming by for a quick fling, though at this point Padraig doubted that anybody watching him was that dumb.

He could still hope.

And he'd talked to himself earlier while scanning, just in case any hidden device was only triggered by sound.

So far, so good.

She moved to the chair. He felt like pacing, but he'd also spent a lot of the day sitting down, first with Brina Jenker and later at Antonov's.

"I might have some better idea of Monsanch," Zarah said.

He nodded for her to proceed.

"If they could distill stubborn and bottle it, they'd be rich around here," Zarah nodded back. "Their founding myths and legends wrap around the single hero, arriving at the moment of greatest need to drive off faceless corporations."

"Samurai?" he asked.

"Close enough," Zarah replied. "They actually have an archetype of a man on a horse, riding an open grasslands while tending herds of grazing beasts, usually armed with a primitive firearm using an explosive propellant, but the tropes run extremely parallel to the samurai. Or at least the bushi/ronin, as most of them tend to be lovable scoundrels, ship captains on small tramps who function as smugglers on the side, but rise above themselves when it comes time to save the day."

"Interesting," Padraig replied.

He quickly gave her a run-down of his meeting with Brina, then his amazing lunch, then the walk with Jamy Hesell.

"And we still think *Traisa* might have done it?" she asked with a gasp when he was done. "To their own ambassador?"

"That's the piece of the puzzle that sticks out with a sharp edge," he told her. "Everyone has reasons to lie to us, but their stories have all generally been consistent. If this is a conspiracy, then everyone else is in on it and keeping their stories straight while they talk to us. If so, we're going nowhere fast."

"But it sounds to me like you feel they are all telling the truth?" Zarah asked.

"I didn't order lunch," he grinned. "I asked her what Joshua would have had, and she started delivering plates without another word. He was that well known. And that well liked."

"You call him Joshua, rather than Ambassador Wrezal?" she pressed.

"At this point, I feel like I know the man rather well, even though we shook hands briefly once," Padraig nodded. "He left an indelible mark on a number of people. I hope that Gomez manages to keep that part of Joshua's legacy going. Even if it is only here on Monsanch. A small bit of immortality, and I think the galaxy is a much darker place without him."

"Can we do anything about *Traisa*?" Zarah asked.

Padraig shrugged.

"As Jamy Hesell noted, diplomatic immunity pretty much hamstrings the local police from doing anything, as anyone that they might want to bring in and interrogate can tell them to get stuffed," he said. "Worse, I expect that the new ambassador will bring with them his or her own staff, and our assassin might be sent home on the same ship, getting away entirely."

"That's wrong," Zarah said sharply.

Padraig commiserated.

"I agree," he told her. "However, that's the thing that separates the military wing of things from the diplomatic. They have to have more space in which to operate, because they are a long ways from home, without orders except as they can ask for clarification and get it within a few days or weeks."

"But they can murder someone and get off scot-free?" she asked.

"I'd like to say otherwise," Padraig replied. "It is likely out of our hands. Best I think I can do at present is to prove everyone who didn't do it, so that they are cleared with Hesell."

"What can he do?"

"Not a lot," Padraig agreed. "But this is his planet, so maybe he tells the entire *Traisa* embassy to leave and get replaced at a later date."

"*Traisa* is our ally, though," Zarah pointed out. "Doesn't that help *Wronlori*?"

"*Traisa* is also the farthest away of any of the major players around here," he reminded her. "And possibly the weakest right now, though I have no doubts that they are building up their own fleet as fast as they can. Just like everyone else is doing. This still feels personal."

"Personal?"

"What Gomez said about Eliana Wrezal," Padraig nodded. "How she might have chosen Joshua over the Supreme Autocrat, at least before Torray took power. If she's a widow, where does she go?"

"Doesn't the woman get to decide that?" Zarah asked in a harder voice than a Squire normally used on her Captain, but they were civilians here and he could see the terrible anger in her eyes.

"She's supposed to," Padraig agreed delicately. "We're talking about the Supreme Autocrat of the *Enlightened Tyranny of Traisa*. And love makes people do stupid things."

"You mean lust," Zarah growled angrily.

"Yes, you're right there, Zarah," he nodded. "The locals who knew Joshua loved him. You only have to hear them talk about him to understand that. Even strangers and cooks. But what if he was the impediment to someone getting to Eliana? What if that's why they might have had the man assassinated, when sending him so many light-centuries from home didn't seem to dim his light one iota?"

"Where does that leave her?" Zarah asked.

"I don't know," Padraig admitted. "She's a *Traisan* citizen. I haven't heard anyone say hardly anything at all about her, so she's almost a cipher."

"Did *she* arrange it?" Zarah pressed.

Padraig was taken back by the vehemence in the woman's voice. Somewhere, somebody had said and done something ugly to Zarah Halloran, but now was not the time to delve into that.

Instead, he made a note to have a chat with Shanti Chaudhary, *Marrakesh*'s civilian Counselor and the person generally responsible for the mental health of his crew, to see if she knew. Or needed to.

But Zarah had asked a question. Sharp and pointed.

He thought back to the initial reception, all of a week ago.

"No," he said simply. "When she found out, she screamed in raw terror and fainted. Maybe she's that good of an actress, but I'll assume instead genuine feelings for her husband, considering the lifestyle that the two of them seem to have maintained on Monsanch."

That seemed to calm Zarah a notch. Padraig assumed someone had leveled some ugly, false accusations at her at some point. Raw nerve.

Still, she was a professional. He watched her compartmentalize whatever it was, then return to the business at hand.

"What's next, Padraig?" she asked, voice almost back to normal.

"We have a meeting in a few hours with Skye Bancroft," he

replied. "She's promised us information, though I'm not sure how far behind she might be, given the day you and I have had. I need some down time to relax and prepare. You should do the same."

"Should I remain in here with you?" she asked with a wink of her eye.

He wanted to order the woman to her own quarters, but Padraig understood that they were trying to maintain a cover. Like two lovebirds, with her some local he'd apparently picked up for sexual activities.

Not that she was homely. Merely that she was female.

"Can you remain quiet?" he asked.

"Got a book," she nodded, tapping her messenger bag that he'd ignored up until now.

So did he. Maybe that mystery would help him relax.

What would Skye Bancroft from *Copez* have for him?

29

Padraig had sent Zarah back to her room, but only after two hours of both of them reading in his. So that it looked like they'd been fooling around, then cleaned up.

Something. He wasn't an expert on leading a double life, though he wondered if all of this might eventually turn into a first-class education on the topic.

Only useful if he wanted to become a spy one of these days, instead of commanding starships.

The rap at his hatch had his hand in his pocket, holding the Type Three. He drew it and held the deadly egg down by his thigh as he moved to the door and peeked outside.

Skye Bancroft. Alone. Dressed in a manner that probably looked seductive, low cut in front, tight in the waist and hips, and high enough to show off shapely calves.

Padraig wondered if he'd end up needing to take the woman to bed as part of some cover or intelligence operation. He could enjoy a woman, she just wouldn't be his first choice. Or third. Possibly not even tenth.

Still, he put the Type Three away and undid the bolt. Pulling the door open, he smiled at the woman.

She smiled back.

"I have reservations for two at a nice noodle house on the edge of downtown," she said.

At least things weren't starting off with any sort of three-some. Small victories.

"I'm ready," Padraig replied, stepping forward to close the door and violating the woman's personal space, as she hadn't moved.

As with last night, a quick kiss hello, though she seemed to put more effort into it this time. Like dinner would be foreplay for something greater.

He'd burn that bridge when he got there.

Instead, Padraig slipped to her side and took her arm like they had walked last night. A couple of lovers on a promenade.

Down the stairs and out the front door of the lobby, he had no idea if he was being watched. Being followed.

No, that was wrong.

Padraig assumed several folks following him, possibly like vultures. He simply didn't know who they worked for. Or what they looked like.

Thus, the Type Three. And the personal transmitter that *Marrakesh* could locate from orbit if they needed to.

This might look like a vacation, and he'd almost been tempted to treat it thus, but it was also serious business that had killed a man.

A good man, as far as Padraig had been able to determine.

"Have you had a good day, today?" Skye asked as they walked down the sidewalk.

The weather had improved, clear skies and a warm front in

the last hour or so, so he'd left Brina's cloak in the room. If Skye didn't know, she didn't need to find out from him.

At least not yet.

"I have," he beamed at her, like this was a date and he had Jean-Michele on his arm, before that man had decided that the long gaps when Padraig was away weren't worth the effort of a relationship.

Pity, but nothing Padraig could do about it.

"What did you do?" she asked.

He wondered if she was interrogating him, or genuinely curious.

"I went to Antonov's for lunch," he replied with a smile. "Told the waitress I wanted what Joshua would have ordered. It was simply stunning."

She nodded, still silent. He left off the part where Jamy Hesell had arrived. And breakfast. And several other things.

"You?" he asked her.

"Mostly spent in an office," she nodded. "Digging into various intelligence files and collating them into a coherent whole that I'll provide you later."

"Later?" he asked.

She grinned and nodded, that nervous tic again.

Pillow talk? So be it. She wasn't ugly. Rather attractive, even. It had merely been something like five years since he'd taken a woman to bed.

She snuggled up against him as they walked.

At least this portion of the evening promised to be fun.

30

Padraig walked serenely, enjoying the late afternoon sun and the friendly woman on his arm. There was much to be said for such a thing.

The man stepping out from a doorway as they approached didn't do anything to draw the eye. Medium height if something of a stocky build. Short-brimmed cap slouched down in front a bit. Brown suit that didn't look all that well-tailored.

It was the gun in the man's hand that got Padraig's attention.

"Nothing stupid, Captain," the man murmured as he stopped a meter away.

On his arm, Skye had stiffened, but remained quiet.

"Both of you, into the vehicle," the man nodded towards the street.

Padraig heard the hatch on a ground car open with a clicking thump and glanced over.

Sedan, he thought they were called. Six wheels on the ground. Four doors. Long and low-slung, with a feeling of speed and power about it. Black paint with a gloss. Darkened windows that hid the interior entirely.

"What's going on?" Padraig asked. Still quiet. The man had a gun.

The late afternoon crowd was thin. Not empty streets, but nobody walking along with them.

"Some people want to talk to you, Captain," the man growled. "And your friend here."

She started to tense and the gun was aimed at her. Padraig supposed that he could try to wrestle the barrel away, but a second man emerged from the land vehicle, also armed.

"Just talk?" he asked.

"That's right," the man said.

"You could have called on me at the hotel," Padraig grimaced.

The man shrugged and nodded to the vehicle.

"We're doing this my way," he commanded. "You first, then the woman."

Padraig nodded, trying to keep everyone calm. There had been no threats, beyond leveled pistols.

Hopefully, this was just someone who didn't feel comfortable talking in public.

He could hope.

"Okay," Padraig said, relaxing. "Moving to the car."

He kept Skye's arm clamped against his side as he moved, drawing her after him in case she wanted to do something that probably sounded heroic in her head and was more likely to end up with one or both of them getting shot.

Monsanch hadn't struck him as a bad place. Iconoclastic, maybe, but understandable.

The second man moved to one side. Padraig got by him and ducked into the car. Facing seats around an empty center, like a shuttle craft made for senior officers might have done it. Nice leather on the seats. He dropped in and slid across facing rear.

There was a third man, also armed, facing forward.

Skye ended up in the middle, then the other two got in, all three facing forward and armed as the doors locked and the vehicle pulled away from the curb.

"Where are we going?" he asked in a polite, curious tone.

"You'll see," the first man replied with a hostile growl.

Yes, he supposed he would.

At least he still had his gear on him.

For what it might be worth.

31

Nyssa looked at what the system had spit out. High probability of accuracy. Coherent message that came out of the hash of jumbled characters and noise.

It was the message that left her chilled to her soul.

She was in an office not that far from the bridge. Not that she'd needed isolation, but it had helped her mindset as she focused on things that made her feel more like a spy and less like a naval officer.

If they were different. Radio Officers handled this sort of thing routinely. Just not at this level of complexity. Or threat.

She reread the message. Cursed under her breath. Saved everything and shut the console down.

Rising, Nyssa moved to the main corridor, then entered the bridge.

Andrea Whelan, Coxswain of the Boat itself, was sitting in Captain Boru's chair, apparently in charge right now as it was late afternoon ship time and they were down a few folks.

The Cox'n was in her mid-forties. Senior-most enlisted

crewmember on *Marrakesh*. Expert at damned near everything after twenty-five years in uniform.

Good woman to have in charge.

Whelan looked at Nyssa with a single, arched eyebrow as Nyssa entered and moved to her normal station. Glen Tameron was sitting watch right now, but Bex was probably still on duty aft. He looked at her for a cue.

She shook her head for him to stay, but reached across him to the spot on his console where a big rocker switch was covered with a cage that took her a moment to snap open. She'd never had a need to do this.

Nyssa flipped the cage open, then the switch.

Red lights came on everywhere and a triple siren sufficient to rouse the dead sounded in every chamber on *Marrakesh*.

Everyone, everywhere, would be racing to their duty stations. She gestured for Glen to stay in place because she would need to brief Commander Messier first, and that might not happen here.

Nyssa wasn't entirely sure what happened next, because she'd never done this before. Any of this. She didn't have to have all the answers.

Messier arrived first. Not wearing shoes, as she slid to a rest next to the Cox'n, who was all set to bail out of the station. Nyssa fixed Whelan with a hard gaze that spiked the woman to the station.

"I need to brief you and Nevin immediately, sir," Nyssa said as folks continued to pile into the bridge at a dead run. "The captain has been kidnapped, down on the surface, and I think the folks who have him mean him harm."

There. Succinct. Complete enough to draw a first level approximation. And to justify sounding the alert, though Nyssa wasn't sure how they would respond.

She was also the youngest officer on board and the third youngest crew member.

She didn't have to do it all.

Nyssa had the entire *A'Zedi* navy backing her up.

She might need them.

32

Chance studied the young Squire. Nyssa might really be the smartest person she knew, but you'd never realize it, looking at the buzz cut hair, the slender build, the dark eyes.

She spoke with utter conviction, though.

"In my office," Chance ordered. Then she turned to Andrea Whelan. "Have the Air Boss warm up both birds and have Lead Farrell round up enough security teams for both, plus two officers to accompany."

"On it," the Cox'n replied, but Chance was already following Taggart to the side office where Padraig normally worked when he wasn't seated in the middle of the bridge.

Where she'd taken over while he was gone.

Temporarily, damnit.

Taggart moved to the desk and brought the screen live. Chance moved to this side of the desk and let the woman work.

"I intercepted a strange message a couple of hours ago, sir," Taggart began. "Burst transmission. Encoded but on a single band. I don't know why it stood out to me, but it did. And we'd have missed it if *Marrakesh* was keeping a standard, high-altitude orbit."

"Luck is a thing I'm happy to exploit," Chance reminded her.

Taggart nodded and gestured her close. Chance rose again and read the message, her jaw dropping as she did.

"I don't know where this place is that they are taking the captain," Taggart noted. "Merely that two groups are coordinating to kidnap him off the streets of Ilham and transport him there. I can't tell because the unit stopped transmitting immediately afterwards."

Chance nodded.

"Do we know who they are?" she asked.

Taggart shook her head.

"I have two call signs, but presumably that's sufficient for them," the Squire said. "There was nothing else I was able to determine. And I was really only able to crack this one because they used Captain Boru's name three times in the message. The cryptographic system keyed on that and broke it outwards from there."

Chance grinned.

"You do realize that there's probably nobody else on this boat that could have done that, right?" she asked the younger officer.

Taggart's eyes got big. Then she sobered and nodded.

"Aye, sir," she admitted. "Orders?"

"Who was the man that Padraig met for breakfast?" Chance asked.

Taggart's eyes unfocused for a moment.

"Harley Gomez," Taggart said a moment later. "Some of my notes suggest that he might be something of a local underworld figure, but I can't be sure without more research."

"I need you to find a way to contact him directly over a comm," Chance ordered. "You do that, then get it to me. While you're doing that, Zarah needs to be briefed, if she's about to lead a rescue mission."

Nyssa Taggart swallowed and looked her young age. Halloran wasn't much older, and possibly the less mature of the two, but both were officers. And acted like it.

Chance exited to the main bridge. Red lights everywhere, blinking to remind you of imminent catastrophe, but not for *Marrakesh*.

Maybe only her Captain.

"Cox'n, I am taking command," Chance ordered crisply, as Whelan moved. "Radio, get Squire Halloran on the line. Now."

33

Zarah picked up the beeping transmitter and put her book down.

"Halloran," she said, not due to check in for another hour or so.

In fact, right before dinner.

"Are you alone?" Commander Messier asked first.

Zarah automatically looked up and around the room.

"I am," she replied.

"Captain Boru has been kidnapped by unknown locals, Zarah," Messier told her.

Zarah went cold all over. A hand went into her pocket for the pistol and drew it, more of a security blanket than anything, but what she needed right this moment.

"Okay?" Zarah said.

"I want you mobile immediately," the Commander said. "Armed, but moving towards the starport in case they decide to pick you up as well."

Zarah was on her feet and stuffing the pistol back into her pocket as she located her messenger bag and the few books she'd checked out. Everything else could wait until later. Or be replaced.

"In motion, Commander," Zarah replied.

"Good," Messier said. "I'm sending down a security force under Armiger Nevin. You will rendezvous with them while Nyssa Taggart tries to determine where they've taken Captain Boru. At that point, your combined force will lead a rescue effort. Nevin will be in charge, but you have the greater experience with the local culture so he has been ordered to listen. Questions?"

"None immediately, sir," Zarah replied, thinking back to conversations about samurai warriors.

Or whatever this was about to turn into. Monsanchers liked to think about cowpokers, or something.

Close enough for government work.

"Check in when you get to the starport, Squire," Messier ordered.

"Understood, sir. Out."

Zarah cut the line and stuffed the transmitter into her pocket instead of the bag, in case she had to drop the bag in a mad scramble. It and the pistol. Nothing else really mattered.

She slipped her shoes on and moved to the door, drawing the pistol anyway and keeping it low to her side. Zarah was qualified with it. All officers had to be as part of their commissioning, because they might serve a stint as a Security Squire on a larger ship, or command such troops on a ground installation.

She'd never once fired in anger. Never even fired outside of a climate-controlled shooting range.

Zarah wondered if that was about to change.

Peeking through the door, nobody was visible as far as the

fisheye would reveal, so she took a deep breath and opened it as quietly as possible.

Nobody.

She moved to the back staircase, simply because the front felt like the easiest way to set a trap. She'd come and gone through the lobby routinely over the last day.

Let's make them guess.

The back door let onto a side street and a parking lot, neither particularly full at the moment. Sidewalks were starting to get busy, but it was that point in the afternoon when folks had gotten off work, made it home long enough to eat, then were heading back out for a vid or a club.

Something to relax.

Zarah didn't figure she'd be relaxing again for a while.

Instead, she walked with a firm tread back in the direction of the tram station, head not on a swivel but watching everything around her like a hawk.

With that deadly egg in her right hand.

34

Maddox couldn't help himself, so he simply moved to parade rest and held it, like Commander Messier was a Fleet Marshal inspecting her troops.

They were in the Captain's ready room. He'd read the communications between the two groups, arranging to capture the Captain and transport him somewhere for interrogation.

Didn't sound promising.

Commander Messier was eyeballing him as she finished her briefing. Not much. Not yet.

"You have an encrypted transmitter and an Adjustable Disruptor," Messier reminded him. "Lead Farrell will have a Disruptor Bombardier, as will half of her team, plus a single Light Disruptor Cannon. I'd prefer you not end up blowing up half the city, Maddox. At the same time, I'd rather you had all the tools you needed on hand, rather than wishing or waiting. Taggart suggests that the Captain might be in more serious trouble than merely someone wanting a private conversation and having poor manners about it. I can always apologize later.

If necessary. You will treat this as a hostile situation until you determine otherwise. Questions?"

Maddox considered everything she'd told him. The few tidbits he'd picked up over the last week, largely watching the evening news from the capital.

"No, sir," he replied. "Playing it by ear, and I understand that there are a lot of bad choices in front of me, so I have to be careful."

"Don't shoot the governor, or one of the other ambassadors," Messier said in a cold, hard voice that Maddox had never heard from her before. "Past that, if someone provokes you, I expect you to defend yourself accordingly. Someone didn't learn any manners as a child, so they get to deal with the *A'Zedi* navy, and we take care of our own. Taggart will update you as she goes."

Maddox swallowed past a lump in his throat and nodded.

"Dismissed," she said with a nod.

Maddox nodded back and broke into a jog. Every second might count, and they still had a lot of kilometers to cover.

Didn't take long to get to the flight bay. Lead Expert Farrell was already there, standing next to the hatch for *Flight of Fancy* as he arrived.

"*Roadrunner* is already descending," she said, moving to the hatch. "I figured that I'd ride down with you, then we'd sort out the teams on the ground."

"Very good," Maddox said automatically, years of training making certain things so automatic that they were unconscious.

Nobody knew what was coming, so they'd asked how high on the way up when the Commander said to jump.

That was life in the navy. And it was a good life.

He just wished, as the hatch sealed and the ship started to move, that it wasn't necessary to send a rescue mission for the Captain.

35

Padraig had gotten frisked when they got to the...barn? Garage? Whatever it was.

The windows in the ground car had been dark enough to make it hard to see out. Large structure had swallowed them like a whale. Folks had gotten him and Skye out of the car and taken his pistol and transmitter, laughing coarsely as they did, but never forgetting to keep several guns pointed at him in the process.

Right now, he was alone in a small, empty room. The door was locked. The walls were made of metal painted the most hideous neon green shade Padraig thought he'd ever seen. Rang like metal when he rapped it with his knuckle, though nowhere as thick as a hull.

The hatch didn't have any handles on this side. Just a lock that had slammed shut with a thump like an emergency bulkhead sealing off a catastrophic leak on the ship.

Weirdly, nobody had asked him any questions. Nor hardly commented. Shuffled him in here and closed the door.

He and Skye had been separated silently and efficiently, with her put somewhere else.

No threats, either, but Padraig didn't know how to qualify that.

Hopefully, when he failed to contact the ship in two more hours, someone would raise an alarm.

Would they be able to track his transmitter? Or was it being taken somewhere else and abandoned?

Padraig paced the back wall, farthest away from the hatch. There were no cameras in here that he could see, so he didn't know if they were watching or not. He had no chair to sit on. Nothing.

Just cubic volume and his thoughts.

What happened next?

36

Nyssa reviewed her logs, back in that side office where she'd worked all afternoon.

Monsanch wasn't a particularly advanced place, though Ilham seemed to be a nice city. Technological enough for her needs.

She started by pointing some of her new tools at the local information network itself. Found an electronic bulletin board fairly quickly that had the name Harley Gomez on it.

Huh, he was going to throw a wake for the *Traisa* Ambassador. Contact him directly for information at this number, because it was going to be a private event, but all of Wrezal's friends should make sure they told each other so that it was huge.

Nyssa located the contact information and paused. Technically, she should get Messier's approval for the next various steps, because some of what she was about to do would be classified as crimes on *A'Zedi* worlds. And probably Monsanch.

On the other hand, she didn't have time. And Messier

could always throw her to the wolves later. After she'd helped rescue the captain.

Nyssa nodded to herself with a hard scowl at the galaxy and started ordering that computer on the ground to let her in.

It wanted to resist, but didn't have a navigation computer behind it. Nor the cryptographic tools she'd dug up from behind high-security clearances here on the ship. Or adapted on the fly today.

The gateway surrendered after a brief struggle, now classifying her with local administrative privileges. Apparently, nobody had ever attempted to brute-force their way into such systems that they would have defended against someone throwing fifty million access requests at it in ten seconds.

Probably still thought that they were the frontier, when Monsanch was more on the verge of becoming a place.

The cursor on the screen blinked politely at her. *Marrakesh* was in low orbit, so the lag was tiny.

She found a menu tree and located the transmitter she wanted from the various communications towers that could all ping it to triangulate.

Downtown. She overlaid a map of Ilham with a few more keystrokes.

Either the unit was in an upstairs office, or more likely it was currently on the ground floor in a particular bar, based on the matching physical address.

Nyssa told the system to connect her to the number.

It rang. After several rings, it went to a voice box to leave a message.

She hung up and looked for local emergency protocols for Monsanch and Ilham in particular.

There.

Nyssa keyed a few of them in, and suddenly, she was operating with equivalent authority to the governor himself, during a declared planetary emergency.

The comm at the other end didn't ring. Instead, it should have beeped loudly three times, then gone live.

"What the hell is...?" a man's voice rumbled.

"I need to speak with Mister Harley Gomez immediately," Nyssa said, pitching her voice like her mom used to do when dealing with a recalcitrant teenager.

"Who are you?" the voice asked.

"This is an emergency," she snapped. "Put Gomez on the line."

There was a pause. Nyssa wondered if he would hang up on her. If so, she might be able to activate every comm within twenty meters and broadcast her annoyance at the man until he talked to her.

That, or vectored Maddox and Zarah down on his head to arrest him. With two security teams that probably weren't feeling particularly charitable right the moment.

The pitch of the audio changed.

"This is Harley Gomez," the voice said, annoyed but quieter. Possibly up against the side of his head instead of using the general speaker she'd activated. "Who is this?"

"I am Squire Taggart, aboard the *A'Zedi* Tactical Transport *Marrakesh* in orbit," she said deliberately. "I need your help, Mister Gomez. That, or I will have to activate the entire planetary militia."

A small part of her, buried deep behind her mission and her need, was appalled that she really could call out every able-bodied person on the planet with access to some of the tools she'd unlocked. At some point, these people needed better information security.

Not today.

ing 2
ned

"What the hell is going on?" Gomez asked.

Nyssa could hear some noise in the background. It sounded like a bar returning to normal as folks began to ignore Gomez. Hopefully.

"Approximately one hour ago, unknown assailants kidnapped my captain off the streets of Ilham, Mr. Gomez," she informed the man. "Rather than contact the governor, Commander Messier instructed me to see if the underworld might help, based on your friendliness earlier."

"Shit. WHAT?"

Nyssa repeated the information.

"Son of a bitch," Gomez muttered. "Boru?"

"That's right," Nyssa said. "I have forces in flight now, but they do not know where to go to locate and retrieve the Captain. He has spoken highly of you. Will you help?"

She waited. It was a risk, if he was behind the kidnapping.

At the same time, she could locate the man easily enough. Send Maddox after him in person.

Or the entire planetary militia, with orders to arrest the man on sight.

Captain Boru's transmitter had stopped pinging, so she could only hazard a guess as to where he'd been up to a certain point, and nothing since. Had they moved him? Broken the device?

She didn't know. And she wasn't bluffing with Gomez.

He could help. Or attempt to hinder.

"Let me make some calls," Gomez replied. "Can I reach you at this number?"

Nyssa considered where she was calling from. Planetary Emergency Operations. Someone might notice if the line went live.

She sent him a different line. One that would automatically

bounce straight up to *Marrakesh* without possibly sounding every storm siren in the city in the process.

"I'll let you know," Gomez acknowledged and cut the line.

Nyssa leaned back and sucked a breath to the depths of her soul before releasing it.

Then she composed a compact message to update the Commander. And Maddox's team.

37

Padraig heard the locks thunk open as he paced, but remained next to the far wall. So far, there had been no threats. Just force.

That same blocky kidnapper flung the door all the way open until it banged against the wall, then stood there with a pistol in hand.

"Good," he announced. "Boss wants to talk to you. This way."

The man stepped back.

Padraig considered his options. Weren't many. Most seemingly ended up with him getting shot.

Not his preferred outcome at present.

He moved to the door, noting that there were two other goons with the first man. Neither had a weapon out, but that just meant that they could grab him and hold him if the first had to get involved.

They took up positions on either side and indeed grabbed his arms. Not twisting. Just holding. Guiding.

The volume outside turned out to be a warehouse of some sort. Long, flat roof overhead with a crane that ran on parallel tracks to lift heavy objects. Most of the floor was open, with a few rusty shelving units that felt roughly five meters tall at the far end. A whole series of garage doors were all closed. Several were marked as inaccessible from the inside.

His cell had been the first of a half-dozen rooms running along this edge of the building. The next two were closed. A light emerged from the open fourth door.

The kidnapper led him there and entered.

There was a chair in the middle of the room, and a handful of gruff-looking men in badly-fitting suits beyond that. Most of them were openly armed.

"Sit," the kidnapper ordered.

A heavy hand pushed him down, then the other two held him. It was like accelerating for liftoff with a two-G pressure holding you to the seat. Not impossible to move around, but things had to be deliberate.

And he was outnumbered more than a dozen to one. With them armed.

Two men emerged from behind the group over there. Older. One was perhaps in his fifties, and had the look of a dandy when he came into view. Almost pretty. Dapper emerald suit. Clean shaven. Slender and tall, accentuated by excellent tailoring.

Pleasant-looking chap, in almost any other circumstances.

The second was harsher. Devil to the first one's angel.

Gray suit cut severely. Graying Van Dyke that served to make his face look more like a hatchet. Or the face of a hammer. Rough skin. Rough hands. Broad build, like they'd carved him out of an oak tree then animated it.

Forty-something, but they'd been hard years on a harder man.

The pretty one spoke first.

"We understand that you are poking around into whoever killed Joshua Wrezal," he announced in a deep tenor that sounded like he should be reading the evening news.

Padraig shrugged. Tried to shrug. Heavy weight on both shoulders kept him immobile.

"That's correct," he offered. "Governor Hesell felt like the police weren't going to be able to do anything more than they had, and asked me to see what I could find out."

"And?" the man in gray next growled like a generator losing a set of bearings.

Padraig considered his words carefully, uncertain if he'd accidentally kicked over some rock and surprised the cockroaches underneath. And if they bit.

"And I've discovered that the man had a lot of friends," Padraig replied. "I've spoken with a number of folks over the last day, and so far nobody has had anything bad to say about Joshua."

He left it at that. Creator's honest truth.

Still, cockroaches?

He studied the two men. Committed their faces to memory, in case he needed to hunt them down and *have a chat* later.

Then he grinned to himself at the thought of taking all these armed men on by himself, with his bare hands.

In the best traditions of the *A'Zedi* navy, he would, if called upon. Maybe by bringing along his own small army of goons.

Hopefully, it wouldn't come to that.

"What is it that you find so entertaining, Captain?" the pretty one asked.

"Governor Hesell wondered if the mere act of my asking around would cause folks to emerge from the shadows who might have otherwise remained hidden and *unsuspected*," Padraig replied evenly. Neutrally.

Lacking any commitment to the topic, as it were.

Merely conveying information.

Still, the two men looked sharply at each other and some silent conversation took place.

Must have been good, from the way their two faces convulsed. Pretty boy suddenly seemed angry enough to chew nails.

The two leaned in close to each other and some whispered conversation occurred, but Padraig only got angry and gruff hisses.

He concentrated on his breathing.

Felt like he'd found an opening he could exploit.

Cockroaches.

Pretty boy suddenly gestured to one of the men behind Padraig.

"Get her," he ordered. "Bring her here."

Padraig assumed they meant Skye, and wondered if she had already been interrogated. And what she'd told these two men.

Must have been fancy lies, from the way they were reacting to Padraig's honest truths.

He waited.

Footsteps announced a return. Several people.

He recognized the clicking of Skye's heels on the concrete floor.

"What's going on?" Pretty Boy demanded. "Boru here tells me that it's all a set-up for Hesell to get names. Our names."

Pretty Boy sounded angry. Man in Gray looked like a rabid badger getting ready to maul something.

Maybe everything.

Padraig looked over his right shoulder as Skye came into view.

And blinked.

Skye Bancroft had a pistol held negligently in one hand.

She smiled at him as Padraig reconsidered many things.

Nyssa Taggart had thought *Traisa* did it. Of course, Skye Bancroft was a spy. A person who told lies and lived double lives for a living.

How many people was she really working for?

"Of course it was a fishing expedition, you idiots," she turned and told the two men. "Your job was to muddy the waters. I can see that such a simple task might have been too complicated for you, though."

"What about him?" Pretty Boy pointed at Padraig now.

"Your instructions were to find out what he knew," Bancroft's voice had turned cold. "I expected more serious efforts on your part, gentlemen. I suppose I'll have to do it myself, then?"

Padraig's head was still spinning. Bancroft, maybe working with the *Traisa* folks? Or had they expressed a need and she'd answered the call? Along with one or two gangs of folks who felt like senior players in Ilham's underworld? Maybe Monsanch's?

"I didn't sign up for this." Pretty Boy's scowl marred his beauty.

She started to say something—snarl it really from the look on her face—then caught herself short.

Bancroft turned to the three goons that had been holding Padraig in place.

"Put him back in his cell," she ordered.

And not one of them complained. Instead, they pulled him

roughly to his feet, then out into the main warehouse and back down to his former cell, shoving him in.

The door locked and Padraig was finally afraid.

What were the odds that he wasn't supposed to get out of this one alive?

38

Nyssa answered the line the instant it rang.

"Taggart," she said.

"It's Harley," he replied. "I got good news and bad. Called in some favors and got you an address. Think that's where your captain is being held."

"And the bad news?" she asked.

"Folks that are doing this shouldn't be this stupid," Gomez replied. "Someone's got their arm twisted up behind them pretty hard and I don't know who or why. I might be able to talk to them, but they're going to want some official cover if shit's about to go sideways. More than you, *Marrakesh*."

Nyssa considered her options. Maddox should be on the ground by now, parked at the starport but still aboard while they sorted out where to go next.

That was her job.

"Harley, I'm going to hang up and call someone else to see what I can do to protect you and your friends," she said. "Don't go far."

"You got it, kid."

Nyssa cut the line and cycled to a different file. She had the number, but it was marked *For Emergencies Only*.

This qualified.

Before she connected, though, she altered the outbound identification transponder code that would go with it. Then put the call on speaker to the bridge, just so Commander Messier could listen in.

And hang her later if Nyssa messed up.

Governor Jamy Hesell answered on the second ring.

"*DC Marrakesh?*" he asked, confused.

"This is Squire Nyssa Taggart aboard *Marrakesh*, Governor," she replied. "I don't have a lot of time to explain, but there is a situation going on, down on the surface, and I need your immediate assistance."

There was a pause. Sounded like the man taking a drink of something and putting it down.

"Okay, Taggart," he said, a man used to command. Like the Captain. "Explain."

Nyssa took her own breath.

"Captain Boru was apparently kidnapped by unknown agents roughly two hours ago, sir," she began. "I have used tools at my command to reach out to locals who can help us, but they fear subsequent prosecution for certain activities if their names were to come to light. They specifically asked me to intercede with you, that you might exercise judicial mercy in their cases, when the truth became known."

She stopped there. Sharp. Precise. Complete, without giving anything away.

"Boru?" he asked. "Someone has him, and someone else will help, but doesn't want to go to prison for their part in helping you?"

"In a nutshell, Governor, yes," Nyssa said. "I told them that I would ask you to help directly."

"That's it?" he asked. "That's all you're asking?"

Nyssa considered her next words. And her career, which she was probably putting on the line. Possibly her freedom, but this whole mission to Monsanch was supposedly protected by rules on diplomatic immunity.

At least until someone figured out what she'd done to their communications network.

"I have a security team in motion right now, Governor," she continued, casting the dice in her head. "They will be attempting a rescue, but that might get messy and out of hand, depending. He's our captain and they are likely to exercise excessive force if they feel it is necessary. Your benevolence now might mean that violence might not be necessary."

"And you don't trust my police forces to assist?" he asked.

"Do you, sir?" she countered sharply. "I had the impression from my captain that they might be considered too corrupted to trust in this matter. My team on the ground are all *A'Zedi* sailors. And trustworthy."

Again, a pause.

"Okay, Squire," Hesell relented. "I like Boru, and he seems to have an exceptional team. I'll back your play and make sure that certain bad elements are allowed to slink away if they help you. I will expect a complete and detailed briefing from you when this is done."

"On my honor, Governor," she said. "Thank you."

She cut the line and dialed Harley. The bridge was still listening.

"What've you got for me?" he asked immediately.

"The Governor is willing to overlook certain actions today and tomorrow, Harley," she said simply. "Your name will have to come up, but as a friendly, helpful citizen, Mr. Gomez. Nothing else. Your friends should be able to escape sanction, as long as nothing happens to the captain."

"I can't promise you anything, *Marrakesh*," Gomez replied. He gave her an address that was on the western edge of Ilham. Industrial and warehouse district. "I'm going to send some messages now, so don't kick in the door until I call you back, okay?"

"Understood, Mr. Gomez," Nyssa said.

He cut the line and she sent Maddox and Zarah a note with the address and instructions to get close, then hold for her orders.

Her orders? Shit, she probably was in charge right now. At least until she could get Commander Messier back up to speed.

The hatch opened and the Commander entered, face serious.

Nyssa started to speak, but Messier waved her to silence.

"Well done, Nyssa," she said.

Nyssa felt the weight of the ship slide off her shoulders, but her job wasn't done yet.

39

Maddox read the note from Nyssa and considered. Move to a location quietly and hold, prepared to unleash violence but not immediately moving to battle.

Sounded like the navy. Six months of boring patrol followed by an hour of utter terror. Or a day, like when that damned Leviathan that had chased them.

Until Captain had put paid to them and chased them back. That was why he was here. Could've died out there. Captain had brought everyone home safe.

Time to do the same for him, because the navy never left one of their own behind.

He turned to Zarah, who had joined them on the ground. *Flight of Fancy* was a little crowded, but sailors were used to worse, normally hotbunking in smaller spaces.

"How well do you know the city?" he asked her, grinning because she'd been down for all of a day at this point.

She grinned back, but turned it into a grimace.

"Well enough to know that we can't move through town with this level of firepower and not have somebody call the cops," she gestured to Farrell and the others. "Plus, Nyssa gave us an address to go to, not a place to hide."

She turned to the pilot.

Air Boss Rafferty.

"Rafferty, bring up a map of the city from where you've overflown it," she said.

Bodies shifted around, mostly folks returning to the fold-down jumpseats they'd previously ridden in to free up space. Maddox followed Zarah forward to look over the Air Boss's shoulder.

"Zoom the upper left quadrant," he said.

Zarah slipped into the empty co-pilot seat and tapped the screen. The address showed a large warehouse in the middle of dozens of others, all identical.

"There are parking lots out front of all of them that are big enough to land, but let's assume that we shouldn't do that unless we're going in firing," he said.

"Agreed," Zarah nodded.

He watched her adjust the screen until a dark spot appeared.

"What about this park?" she asked. "It's night, so the parking lot should be empty, and it puts us close enough to move overland. Worst risk is that someone calls the cops and reports us, causing them to show up."

"Nyssa's message suggested that she was pretty deep in their local comm systems," Maddox suggested. "Suppose she could intercept those calls?"

Zarah turned and looked hard at him for a moment, then turned back and tapped a button on the console.

"*Marrakesh*," Nyssa Taggart replied immediately.

Maddox listened as Zarah gave the address.

"If we landed there, could you short-circuit locals from calling the cops?" Zarah asked.

"Stand by," Nyssa replied. "Yes, make sure you come in from the southwest, largely following that creek bed at one thousand meters, then drop hard and fast, getting on the ground and going quiet and dark. I've taken control of a set of junction boxes and anyone attempting to call an emergency line will come here first. We'll triage and reroute them on the fly."

Maddox let go a low whistle. For someone so young, he'd always known she was smart, but was willing to admit a previous bit of resentment that she'd been directly commissioned from the enlisted ranks, rather than coming up through Naval University like the rest of them.

He was also now willing to admit she'd earned it.

Zarah looked up at him and Maddox nodded.

About a kilometer away, but the warehouses should swallow all that sound and keep anyone over there from hearing a pair of shuttles. Then they could overland it close, staying to side streets and hopefully not looking like an invading army.

Regardless of the reality.

"Understood, Squire," Maddox replied.

As Armiger, he was in charge down here, at least until they got the captain back.

"Okay, I've set up a flight plan for you and cleared it with local flight operations," Nyssa said, causing Maddox to blink. And Rafferty as well.

"You can do that?" they both asked in harmony.

"These people do not secure their government systems with anything like a quality lock," Nyssa replied. "Begin your move now, then stand by for my local contacts to clear you. *Marrakesh* out."

The line went dead. Maddox nodded. That woman had her shit together.

Might mean the difference tonight.

"Air Boss, get us up and over, then set us down," Maddox said. "Halloran, you stay up here."

He moved back to his own jumpseat next to Security Lead Farrell and buckled himself in as the engines started to power up and whine.

Next stop, rescuing the captain.

40

Nyssa had already brought the ship to red alert earlier, so Secondary Bridge was fully staffed. Plus, she'd gone ahead and grabbed everyone qualified to sit a Radio watch.

The park and surrounding neighborhood where *Roadrunner* and *Flight of Fancy* had gone was fairly upscale. Expensive real estate facing onto a greenbelt park and creek that ran southeast before joining the larger river near downtown.

Fewer emergency calls had come in than she had expected, and many of those were apparently rich folks calling for the police to investigate suspicious people moving around, rather than active crimes or medical situations.

Some quiet part of her brain had known that would be the case when she'd ordered them to overfly this neighborhood.

Still, everything was being handled aft, leaving her free to monitor. She picked up immediately when Harley Gomez called.

"*Marrakesh*, this is Taggart," she said.

"Harley," he replied. "I've got someone inside who will help a little, but he's surrounded by folks that he can't talk to, because there are parts of three different gangs in there right now, and everyone's a little touchy. Like a pack of dogs confined, ya know? Not sure how much he can do, at least until things go sideways."

"Understood, Mr. Gomez," she said. "I'll move my teams into place and see how they would go about assaulting the place. We'll have medical staff available to keep casualties to a minimum if possible. Will we be able to identify friendlies inside?"

"Captain Boru will, once you get to him," Harley said. "Past that, there's not a lot I can do in the time we have available, because my friend thinks that things are likely to get out of hand soon. Your people should move as quickly as possible. I'm sorry, I wish I could do more."

"You've done a tremendous amount, Harley," Nyssa said. "We'll take it from here."

"Good luck, kid," and he cut the line.

Nyssa changed channels.

"*Flight of Fancy*. Rafferty."

"I need Armiger Nevin," she said.

"Nevin here."

"There will be insiders when you get there, who may be able to help," she explained, detailing what Harley had told her. "You should move in, identify things, and prepare to assault the facility quickly, as he didn't know what their intentions were. Merely that time was burning short."

"Understood, *Marrakesh*," Maddox replied. "We're in motion now and will check in when we get to the warehouse. Out."

Nyssa cut the line and leaned back, blowing out a hard breath.

Would it be enough?

41

Padraig squared up as the door unlocked, but didn't try to rush it. Up until now, the people holding him had shown professional care. And excessive firepower.

As before, the door swung all the way open to slam noisily against the wall. The first kidnapper stood there. The Man in Gray stood beside him, still looking like a hungry predator prepared to savage someone.

"He's dangerous," the kidnapper announced.

Man in Gray turned to the man with a scowl of disdain that actually caused the kidnapper to flinch.

"So am I," the Man in Gray snarled. "You stay out here."

He stepped into the room and slammed the door shut with enough authority that the building creaked slightly. Then the man turned to Padraig and that hammer face split into a smile.

It was only there for a moment, but it was warm and friendly as the man took a step forward, right hand outstretched to shake.

Padraig wondered, but the man was alone. He couldn't be that deadly, could he?

"Harley Gomez called me," the Man in Gray murmured as he stepped close.

The right hand turned skyward and Padraig realized that his Type Three was in it.

He studied the man with confusion.

The Man in Gray held out the hand to shake. Padraig stepped forward and did, ending up with the weapon in his hand.

"My organization, at least, was sold a pig in a poke, Boru," the Man in Gray said quietly, hardly above a whisper now that they were barely half a meter apart. "I don't appreciate being set up like this, but there are too many folks on the other side of that door for me to start trouble. Not unless I wanted a full firefight in here tonight that did the cops a major favor. You need to get away from here. Right now. Am I clear?"

He nodded to the outside wall, the corner. Padraig understood.

"I'm going to punch you now, Captain Boru," he said precisely. "You end up over there and stay down, so they think I've been beating and abusing you. Since you won't talk, they'll have to figure out what to do next to interrogate you. That will take time. Tell Harley I said hi."

Padraig nodded and watched the Man in Gray shift around to line up a shot. He slipped the pistol into his pocket.

The punch was no worse than he'd suffered in a bar brawl, then the man grabbed him by the jacket and slammed him hard into the wall, causing the whole building to ring like a bell for a moment.

Padraig shook his head to clear it, but he'd been prepared, so no concussion.

The Man in Gray smiled briefly, then his face turned back into that terrible mask.

Padraig stayed on the ground where he'd crumpled, right in the corner, as the big man pounded a mighty fist on the door.

It opened almost immediately. Half a dozen goons stood by with pistols aimed.

"Fool wants to do it the hard way," he announced. "Lock him in while I send the boys for something to make it a memorable sort of event. They don't get to do this that often, so they don't carry that stuff with them."

The Man in Gray stepped to the door, pulling it shut behind him as the men outside with him laughed like a pack of hungry wolves.

42

Padraig studied the situation with new eyes.

Allies, of a sort, but limited. Still, the man had bought him time. And given him a Type Three.

Padraig checked the weapon and it seemed to be in full, working order.

Even on his best day, there was no way to shoot his way through so many gunmen.

Ergo, he needed to go the other way.

Padraig turned to the metal he was leaning against. It was an I-beam, set into concrete, with sheets bolted to it on the outside.

He didn't have machinist's tools, but he did happen to have a hand-held particle cannon. It didn't have the variable aperture of a larger weapon, so it was most effective at under twenty meters.

This room was smaller.

He studied the way things were assembled. Sheet metal. Bolts with the head on the outside of the building and the washer and nut inside with him.

Cheap work, or at least easy to assemble quickly, once you poured a slab and had a skeleton for it.

It did give him an idea.

Padraig rose and moved to the door, flexing his left shoulder where he'd slammed it into the wall pretty good. There'd be one hell of a bruise there later.

He assumed verisimilitude. It certainly had been loud.

The Type Three was a compact weapon. A flattened egg with a trigger on the top for a thumb and a safety underneath you had to simultaneously squeeze to activate the unit.

Padraig wasn't an expert gunman, but he'd heard of a trick in his crazier years. He pointed the beam emitter at the lock mechanism from a distance of about two meters and fired a shot with as much care as painting or baking.

Hit. Hopefully, it hadn't thrown any sparks out the far side, but if he was lucky, he might have just welded the lock mechanism in place to the point that the goons outside could only open the door if they broke the lock out. Or broke the door down.

The sound hadn't been loud, but he assumed that someone might have heard it.

Moving quickly to the corner, Padraig located the bottom-most bolt and fired a shot from much closer. Not quite touching it, because he knew there would be flashback and maybe hot metal shards. Medical could handle that later, assuming he got free today.

The bolt shattered with a tremendous thump that echoed hollowly through the building.

There wasn't much time.

Padraig's second shot was rushed. Instead of hitting the bolt, it chomped a divot out of the I-beam and part of the wall itself.

He wondered what it might have looked like from the outside, but didn't let that slow him down.

The third shot went off as quickly as he could cycle the mechanism.

Again, dull bong that rang through the entire skin of the warehouse.

Someone closed a fist on the outside door handle and tried to turn it, but it held. They screamed at the heat transmitted.

Padraig measured his shots. Ground and up one meter. It would have to be enough.

Pocketing the Type Three to free up his hands, he dropped onto his butt and grabbed the I-Beam as he put his feet on the wall. The metal was warm, but not too hot to hold onto.

He put everything he had into the bottom of the sheet, where two bolts were no longer holding the skin to the frame. The metal was thin enough.

And he was desperate.

A shoulder slammed into the door as someone out there also got desperate.

The metal began to fold, then hands outside grabbed it and began to pull it open. Other hands grabbed his ankles.

43

Maddox studied the warehouse. They had the right address, according to Taggart, plus there were lights on inside, visible from the skylights, when all the rest of them were dark tonight.

Outside lights lit the parking lot, so he had his force down and around the side, looking at a row of garage doors overlooking bays where someone could back up a trailer, plus a couple where someone could drive in directly.

"Sir, you need to see this," Expert Trinh Hoàng said from where she was covering this side of the building, stretched out flat on the asphalt on a tarp, with the Light Disruptor Cannon on a bipod and a scope she had her eye against.

Maddox turned in time to see a big flash of light emerge from the near corner of the warehouse. THROUGH the wall.

Disruptor fire that missed? Felt like it.

"We've just run out of time," Maddox announced. "Everybody move."

Or rather, they needed to catch him, because Maddox was already running. Farrell was next to him. Zarah had been facing the wrong way, but he could hear her as a dozen others got running.

A third flash of light accompanied the sound of metal flexing, right where the first one had been. Maddox centered on that.

"Farrell, cover the nearer door with a team," he said as he ran. "Zarah, cover the other side."

All of the security folks were rated for this sort of work, but only Farrell trained full time. Best if he had three people in command, him in the middle and each of them on a wing.

He had no idea what was coming, except that he'd brought a stupid amount of firepower with him tonight.

The lights were enough to see the wall starting to deform as someone inside started pushing to bend it outwards. Maddox got there quickly and recognized the boots visible. They were identical to his.

"Pull it open and get him out," Maddox ordered. "That's the captain."

Beam fire on his left caused Maddox to duck and look. Someone had just blown a fist-sized hole in the door over there as it opened. One of his people, because Cameron Farrell's barrel was glowing slightly.

"Warning shot," she said with a quick look his direction.

Then Captain Boru was in the clear and somebody lifted him to his feet.

Captain drew Maddox and the others away from the corner he'd opened, looking around and counting more than a dozen noses.

"Orders, sir?" Maddox asked, smiling because he'd mostly feared that they'd get here too late, instead of just in the nick of time.

More fire from the left as Farrell and her folks opened up

on people trying to get out of that door. So far, no bodies were down, but they had no cover here.

Captain Boru had a look in his eyes of a man who really wanted to kick that door in over there and open fire, but it passed as Maddox watched.

A rueful grin replaced it.

"Withdraw at speed," Captain Boru said. "Nobody has been seriously hurt at this point."

"I have a garage door opening on my side," Zarah called. "Do we attack?"

"Negative, Squire," Captain called back. "I don't know who it might be, and there are a few friends inside that I'd rather not hurt if we can avoid it. Only fire if they prove hostile."

"Leapfrog formation backwards," Farrell's loud voice over-rode everyone. "Halloran's team back first, then cover us. Nevin, get the captain to safety immediately."

Maddox wanted to argue, but recognized that she was right. She and Zarah were on the points of engagement, with him suddenly in the soft, safe spot.

Then a black land cruiser emerged from Zarah's door, moving away at high speed, but not before Hoàng put a single bolt into the rear fender, nearly tearing it off.

"Hold fire, Hoàng," Captain Boru yelled, when the vehicle turned away and kept accelerating. "Suppressing fire only."

Maddox had thought that the woman opening up with a Light Disruptor Cannon would be sufficient, but he hadn't taken into account how flimsy the building was. She put her first shot over their heads and a section of the warehouse as big as his chest exploded inwards with a tremendous flash of light and sound.

Maddox watched as Captain Boru laughed and started to jog towards Hoàng's position, a Type Three in one hand.

More shots opened up the building, but all of them were overhead, at least three meters up.

Maddox grabbed his personal transmitter and brought it live.

"Air Boss, this is Armiger Nevin," Maddox said. "Meet us at Position Three for immediate extraction."

"Position Three, aye," Rafferty replied instantly. "Lifting now. ETA twenty-five seconds."

Maddox stretched his legs and passed Captain Boru.

"This way, sir," he said. "Got both boats landing in a nearby parking lot."

"Excellent work, Nevin," Captain said back. "All of you."

Behind them, the other two teams kept up a steady stream of fire, but nobody else had emerged at this point. Maddox had no idea what the interior of the facility looked like, but he imagined that they were all going for corners to hide like rats, though his folks had brought enough firepower to handle it.

Captain Boru was up to something else.

They ran.

44

Padraig had to keep from letting the adrenaline overwhelm him. He had seen that mad gleam in Nevin's eyes, the one that wanted to kick in doors firing. Farrell would be looking forward to it. Hoàng was probably having too much fun for her own good, but he'd known it was her as soon as she'd nearly killed the big sedan that had brought him to the warehouse.

Who it was that might be taking this moment to flee could be any of the three big players, and at least one of them deserved to get away.

"Hold here," Padraig ordered.

Hoàng ceased fire as Padraig came even with her, then stood, slinging the cannon and folding up her tarp in a single motion he knew she practiced relentlessly. Part of qualifying for the big gun, and only her and Farrell were rated to use it.

He got to a corner and paused, glancing back. None of the punks in the warehouse had emerged. None were firing back right now, because they'd have to climb atop some of the inner rooms to shoot out of the sorts of holes the Light Disruptor Cannon had left.

Instead, all of his people were retreating quickly, crab walking with guns pointed at the building. Overhead, he heard both *Roadrunner* and *Flight of Fancy* vectoring in.

Padraig nodded to Maddox Nevin and signaled for the man to start off again, all of Padraig's rescuers surrounding him as they got to the corner and cut diagonally across a parking lot. Two angels were descending from the heavens in a rush of wind and noise.

He followed Maddox to *Flight of Fancy* and went right through the hatch without breaking stride, then bounced off the shorter man as they all madly scrambled for seats.

"Put all weapons on safety," Rafferty announced over a loudspeaker.

Not a bad idea, as hyped as everyone would be.

"What are your orders, Nevin?" Padraig asked.

"We're the relief column, sir," Maddox replied with a grin. "Nyssa's in charge of the operation."

Nyssa??? Interesting.

"Rafferty, get *Marrakesh* on the horn," Nevin continued.

"*Marrakesh*, Taggart."

"Nyssa, we've got the Captain," Nevin said. "He's asking about your orders."

Padraig had himself buckled in. *Flight of Fancy* leapt into the sky a moment later, with the hatch still closing as they did.

"Taggart, who should I be thanking, besides you?" Padraig asked.

"I'll have a list for you, sir," she replied. He could hear the smile in her voice. "Right now, I am contacting the Governor to let him know. Stand by."

Flight of Fancy hit a thousand meters elevation quickly, then headed out flat. Padraig had a good enough view forward to see that they were moving away from the starport, towards the darker parts of the countryside where the lights of individual farms and small towns were all that you saw, rather than the sea of golden fire that marked Ilham.

"Okay, sir, I'm back," Nyssa said after two minutes. "Governor Hesell asks that we meet him tomorrow morning at first light, so I'm vectoring you to *Marrakesh* for now. You'll have five hours aboard ship to nap, shower, and have a medical review before departure again. See you shortly."

Padraig grinned. It seemed infectious, as the others grinned back. Zarah was in the co-pilot's seat when she turned around and he blinked in surprise. Farrell must be aboard *Roadrunner*.

Rafferty stood the vessel on its ass and went almost straight up, engines screaming into the night.

45

Padraig had gone ahead and put on his nicer uniform. He'd wanted to bring Zarah Halloran and Maddox Nevin down, but both had demurred and pretty much ordered him to bring Nyssa Taggart instead. She also wore her better uniform.

Air Boss Rafferty had landed them on a pad at the rear of the government palace compound, then shut down his engines.

"We're here," the man said, but made no effort to unbuckle.

So Padraig had stood, towering some over the much smaller Squire next to him. Physically, she was a small woman, but a change had come over her in the last two days.

HAD IT ONLY BEEN TWO PLANETARY DAYS???

Padraig shook himself once at the amount of things that had happened in that brief period. She looked up at him and grinned, like she was reading his mind and equally amazed.

Padraig moved to the hatch and keyed it open, descending two steps onto a lawn you could bowl on if you wanted to. He paused for Nyssa to catch up and they walked side by side to the rear of the palace, where a pair of guards saluted crisply.

"This way, sir," a man Padraig recognized emerged and bowed.

He had been the aide who had whispered in Governor Hesell's ear, when they first discovered Joshua's body at the reception.

The man led them down a pair of corridors, then through a closed door.

The space was a conference room, but the table only filled this half, leaving the other open.

"The Governor will be with you shortly," the aide said, withdrawing with another bow.

Padraig turned to Harley Gomez, seated at the far end of the table with a mug of coffee in his hand and a huge smile on his face.

He moved towards the man and Gomez rose.

"Really good to see you again, sir," Padraig said as they shook hands.

Gomez nodded to Nyssa.

"I'm here because of her," the man said.

Padraig nodded. He'd gotten the whole story. Nyssa surprised the hell out of both men by stepping up and hugging Gomez.

"Thank you, Harley," she said, nearly vanishing inside his arms.

Gomez wasn't Padraig's height, but might outmass him.

"Kid, I'm still laughing at being one of the good guys," Gomez said as they stepped apart. "If you only knew the truth."

"Oh, I know, Harley," Nyssa laughed. "I had to look you up last night. Governor Hesell has a most interesting and possibly complete dossier on you."

"And he still let me in here?" Harley Gomez laughed with her.

Padraig nodded. He'd gotten highlights from Nyssa last night, and as near as he could tell, Harley Gomez was a fixer.

If you had a problem, you went to him with money, and he *fixed* it. Whatever *it* might be. Legal or not. Usually not.

Padraig still wasn't entirely sure why Monsanch needed such a man. Or why Jamy Hesell let him run around.

Except that he'd been close friends with Joshua Wrezal. That man had had a magical touch.

The hatch opened behind them and everyone turned to see Governor Hesell enter. Alone, interestingly.

He joined them and everyone shook hands, though the Governor of Monsanch apparently didn't rate a hug. Wherever that put him in the hierarchy.

"Sit, please," Hesell said, taking a spot on the near side instead of the head, as Padraig had expected.

He paused to study all three of them for a long moment, moving face to face.

"There have been...*developments* since last night," Hesell began. "Skye Bancroft escaped from the warehouse where you were being held, apparently in the ground car that your team damaged with some sort of artillery, Captain. She was seen entering the *Traisan* embassy compound not long after that, and has claimed political asylum. The Deputy Ambassador confirms it."

"What does that mean in layman's terms?" Padraig asked, a bit uncertain.

He did note that Sana Alkes was not present, when she probably should have been.

Unless all of this was happening off the books. *Sub rosa*, as it were, and Hesell wanted to separate the actions of *Marrakesh* and its crew from the official activities of the *A'Zedi* Embassy.

"Generally, it means that she is safe," Hesell nodded with a vague shrug. "She can stay in the embassy and we cannot touch her. If they issue her diplomatic credentials, she can also leave the planet safely."

"So she gets away?" Nyssa demanded quietly. Angrily. "After all that she did?"

Hesell smiled. It made him look like a predator, which rather fit with the rest of them.

"No," he said simply. "My office is in the process of declaring her and the Deputy Ambassador from *Traisa* as *persona non grata*. The new ambassador is scheduled to arrive in just under seventy hours, so I will give them eighty to depart the planet, with instructions never to return. The new *Traisan* Ambassador will not be credentialed, nor recognized. Instead, they can go home on the ship that carried them here. Most of that embassy will be sanctioned, and all the non-natives will be required to depart as well."

"Isn't that a bit harsh?" Padraig asked, still hoping to prevent this from escalating into a major diplomatic row.

"I've read Squire Taggart's intercepts, Captain," Hesell replied, turning to study Padraig's face. "And know the players and the situation far better than she does. This was a joint effort. Only the fact that the Bishop immediately renounced her when he was informed kept him from going on my list, too. And he understands that I'm not pleased there, so he has to walk a narrow ledge for a while."

"So *Wronlori* comes out ahead?" Nyssa asked. "If everyone else is in trouble?"

"No," Hesell said with a warm smile. "There is a new ambassador from *A'Zedi* that just arrived. She strikes me as eminently qualified and quite interesting, so hopefully she can fill in some of the social gap. As to the rest, I've tasked Harley here with making certain arrangements for an ongoing, monthly party in Joshua Wrezal's honor. I'm told that it was your idea, Captain Boru?"

Padraig watched Gomez blush as the Governor spoke, then turned back to Hesell.

"Not counting Bancroft, and I assume she was probably lying, everyone I have met on this planet that knew him had nice things to say about Joshua, Governor," Padraig nodded. "About how he cut across all social lines, collecting interesting people and introducing them to one another, when they might not meet, otherwise. That shouldn't be allowed to fall off with him gone. Perhaps doubly so."

Hesell nodded.

"Which was why I asked the three of you to meet me here this morning," the man said. "Harley is going to take Squire Taggart to meet some of the folks involved last night, because they demanded it when he told them what she'd done. While that's happening, Captain, I thought you and I might return to Antonov's. I asked last night about your lunch yesterday and had never heard of such a thing. I'm hoping that they can replicate it for us today. Then later, there will be a more formal reception, where Sana Alkes is properly introduced to Brina Jenker and representatives from neither the *Holy Imperium of Copez* nor the *Enlightened Tyranny of Traisa* will be welcome."

"A new start for Monsanch, sir?" Padraig asked, approving.

"Indeed, Captain," he said. "And new friends."

46

Padraig looked around his office with a grin as Chance got settled. It was just the two of them today, after everything that had happened over the last week and change.

"We finally done?" she asked with a tired smile on her face.

It had been a whirlwind, and Padraig had been far deeper into everything than he'd ever imagined when tasked with hauling an ambassador to Monsanch. Plus, with him off the ship so much, Chance had had to handle twice the load up here on the ship.

"I think so," Padraig nodded. "Ambassador Alkes has slid in and hopes to fill some of the gaping holes left by *Traisa* and the *Holy Imperium* being on the Governor's shit list. She's assembling a package of materials for me to haul home. As soon as that arrives, we're set to break orbit, unless you have any last-minute surprises?"

"Nothing here," she shook her head. "Kaitlin is looking forward to having a private, five-star restaurant at her disposal for a couple more weeks, and threatened all of us to remain on our best behavior if we wanted an invitation to dinner."

Padraig laughed. Because of Joshua, he had a much better understanding of cuisine and conversation.

"I think my greatest regret is that I never got to meet the man himself," Padraig mused. "Everyone had such great things to say about him, and he left an enormous footprint on that world's culture. Hopefully Harley can keep it going."

"We ever coming back?" she pressed.

He shrugged.

"Beyond my control," he offered. "We'll go where the fleet sends us. Do whatever missions they have in mind for a ship like *Marrakesh*."

"Just so you are aware that we've done some really crazy shit so far," she pointed out. "As much time as I spent while I was on a desk job with the kids, you've already had more adventure than most captains a decade older than you."

Padraig nodded.

"I've got an amazing crew," he told her. "That includes you. And while I'd like to think that an old Tactical Transport like this shouldn't really be off having adventures, I'm okay with it. Plus, I have no idea what High Command is going to say when they hear about this. I kinda colored outside the lines here."

"Padraig, what you did is literally the definition of *above and beyond the normal call of duty*," she said. "They ought to pin a medal on you and Nyssa, though given the way things went down, somebody might wisely keep that sort of thing quiet. What we were doing was far more like espionage than a normal ship gets up to. I'm just glad I was able to be part of it."

"Me, too," Padraig said. "We've got something special here, and I'd like to keep it as long as possible."

READ MORE

Be sure to read the rest of the Operation Marrakesh series!

https://www.knottedroadpress.com/product-category/science-fiction/operation-marrakesh

ABOUT THE AUTHOR

Blaze Ward writes science fiction in the Alexandria Station universe (Jessica Keller, The Science Officer, The Story Road, etc.) as well as several other science fiction universes, such as Star Dragon, the Dominion, and more. He also writes odd bits of high fantasy with swords and orcs. In addition, he is the Editor and Publisher of *Boundary Shock Quarterly Magazine*. You can find out more at his website www.blazeward.com, as well as Facebook, Goodreads, and other places.

Blaze's works are available as ebooks, paper, and audio, and can be found at a variety of online vendors. His newsletter comes out regularly, and you can also follow his blog on his website. He really enjoys interacting with fans, and looks forward to any and all questions—even ones about his books!

Never miss a release!
If you'd like to be notified of new releases, sign up for my newsletter.

http://www.blazeward.com/newsletter/

Buy More!
Did you know that you can buy directly from the KRP website?

https://www.knottedroadpress.com/shop/

Connect with Blaze!

Web: www.blazeward.com
Boundary Shock Quarterly (BSQ):
https://www.boundaryshockquarterly.com/

ABOUT KNOTTED ROAD PRESS

Knotted Road Press publishes dynamic fiction set in exotic locations and unique non-fiction voices in genres such as autobiography, business, cookbooks, and how-to. Our authors cover a wide range of genres including science fiction, fantasy, mystery, literary, and poetry, appealing to all readers. We offer both DRM-free ebooks and print books for a global readership.

Knotted Road Press
www.KnottedRoadPress.com
www.KnottedRoadPress.com/Shop